Viking Princess

Mary Ruth Reed

Viking Princess

Mary Ruth Reed

Tuckamore Books
a Creative Publishers imprint

St. John's, Newfoundland
2000

©2000, Mary Ruth Reed

Le Conseil des Arts | The Canada Council
du Canada | for the Arts

We acknowledge the support of The Canada Council for the Arts for our
publishing program.

We acknowledge the financial support of the Government of Canada
through the Book Publishing Industry Development Program (BPIDP)
for our publishing program.

Front Cover Art © 2002, Nancy Keating

∞ Printed on acid-free paper

Published by
TUCKAMORE BOOKS
an imprint of CREATIVE BOOK PUBLISHING
a Transcontinental associated company
P.O. Box 8660, St. John's, Newfoundland and Labrador A1B 3T7

Second Printing February 2004

Printed in Canada by:
TRANSCONTINENAL

National Library of Canada Cataloguing in Publication Data

Reed, Mary Ruth, 1928-

ISBN 1-894294-19-X

1. Vikings--Juvenile fiction. I. Title.

PS8585.E657V55   2000   jC13'.6   C00-950114-2
PZ7.R25275Vi   2000

To Nat Reed
with special thanks
and to my sister Jean.

Chapter One

Edith crept cautiously up to the edge of the precipice and peered over. Many times her parents had told her to stay away from the cliff. "You may become dizzy and fall," her father had warned.

How could someone feel dizzy while on solid ground? Yet here she was, lying on her tummy looking over a cliff, and she felt dizzy.

Edith moved away from the edge and rolled onto her back. She gazed up into the bright summer sunlight. A falcon made a great shadow as it swooped across the sky above her. Edith liked the strong spread of the bird's wings, the curve of its talons and beak. How wonderful that there were such interesting things to look at when she was watching over her father's sheep.

Edith was twelve years old but she wished she were sixteen. Sixteen was the age of magic. At sixteen she would be a beautiful woman, tall with hair even paler than it was now.

She got up and walked over to the pool where she washed in the summer time. An angry frown creased her face as she gazed down at her reflection. Her forehead slanted off into the ripples and some parts of her face looked pointed.

"Ah!" Edith said, getting to her feet. She should be busy taking stones from the fields. She knew that everyone in Greenland had to work very hard just to stay alive, for this was a harsh country — not at all like Norway, her parents' homeland.

Neighbours would often visit their family and talk about the wonders of days in the old country — a land where there were both rich and poor. In this new land, everyone was poor. Edith sighed. She loved to hear of Norway's castles and gardens, the feasts and lovely clothes; the snowfalls, bears and wolves . . .

Edith's mother had warned her that such stories grew with each telling, yet in almost the same breath she awed Edith with tales of houses not made of sod, but logs. Edith was amazed to hear of great rooms warmed by huge wood fires. Such waste disturbed Edith, who was proud of finding useful pieces of driftwood to make furniture. In the winter their hut was warmed by burning small bushes from the copse-woods and by heat from whale oil and seal oil lamps.

Ronaald, Edith's older brother, loved dreaming of a land to the west of Greenland called Markland. It was to Markland that the men of the village went to cut their wood. As Edith gazed down a pathway, she saw some men going to the ship; among them she recognized Gunnar, Larus, and Haakon. Gunnar was her father's friend, who told her stories of sea monsters and teased her about not being as big and strong as his daughters. Gruff old Larus was known for his heroism, and princely-looking Haakon the Hateful, was known for . . . well, Edith supposed he was best known for being hateful. "It takes a brave crew to sail from the coast," Edith told the uninterested sheep. "Trading and bringing timber is very dangerous."

She had difficulty believing in places such as Markland. However, if there was no Markland, where did the prized wood come from?

Edith looked up at the late afternoon sun. "I'd better get the sheep into the barn before it gets dark," she told herself. "It would not do to let them stray at night, for they might fall into the sea." The wool clipped from their sheep each spring kept them warm in the winter. The sheep also supplied meat, milk and cheese, and the care of these valuable and willful animals was a trying responsibility.

Edith had just turned the last of the sheep into the barn when Ronaald came running up to her. "Hurry, Edith. There are guests at the house. They are talking of the place called Vineland the Good."

"Shall we listen to such lies?" Edith asked. She counted the sheep and put the bar across the gate.

"Our people have been there," Ronaald said, sounding annoyed. "The Irish have also been there."

Edith tossed her head. "So? And who tells the biggest stories? Our people or the Irish?"

"Is there anything that you believe in?"

"Many things!" Edith stopped and looked up at the sky. "I believe that one day we will walk on the stars. I don't believe we will ever walk in Vineland the Good. I believe in things I can see. I believe in glaciers and in great white bears. I believe in myself. I believe that one day I will be a great leader."

"Rubbish," Ronaald said scornfully.

When Edith arrived home with Ronaald, she said little in front of her mother and father's friends. She was wise enough to know they might laugh, so she sat quietly and listened. There were the same old tales — kings and wars, and riches and ships. It seemed everyone wanted to go exploring.

Edith's father, Valgard, seemed excited by Gunnar's tales, yet never asked to join the sailors. Edith wondered if her father felt as she did, brave when faced by danger, but chilled by the thought of a trip surrounded by water.

Gunnar had never been to Vineland but he spoke of men who had been there. Edith listened to his tales of calm bays with green, peaceful islands and strange plants and food. When Gunnar repeated his much-told tale of a dragon that ate a boat, and a fish that speared a sailor with its own sword, she almost chuckled aloud.

It appeared to Edith that her father felt the same amusement she did, for he slapped his knees in merriment.

"Come, Gunnar!" he said. "Are we to believe this

tall tale? There is no doubt a dragon could break a boat in two with its great jaws but it could not eat it."

"It happened, Valgard," Gunnar insisted. "Dragons possess an enormous internal fire that aids them with their meals. About five years ago my wife's brother saw a dragon take a boat that was next to the one he was in. There was fire and smoke raging from the huge mouth as the ship was devoured. The sailors were pulled from the ocean but all else was crushed and splintered as it was swallowed."

"So these tales are true!" Ronaald said. His eyes were large with excitement.

"Do not heed Gunnar," Valgard told him with a guffaw.

Ronaald is my big brother, Edith thought, yet he believes like a small boy. I wonder, could Gunnar be right? Father is wise and he says it is impossible! I do think Gunnar means only to entertain us.

As she helped her mother prepare bowls of cheese and berries for their guests, she said, "Look at Ronaald! A great boy believing in such nonsense."

"You puzzle me," her mother said. "You believe in Norway, Iceland and Ireland, but not Markland and Vineland, even though they are nearer."

Edith was not troubled by her mother's words. At least doubting means I am grown up enough to have my own opinions, she thought.

As the evening wore on Edith shrank further and further into her corner of the hut. Surely things would always be the same in her boring little village. She would always herd sheep, and spin and weave, and she would always pick up rocks from her father's fields.

She glanced over at her brother. Ronaald's eyes glowed as he listened to the adults talk of the ship that was anchored in their fjord. It had oars for thirty men.

Ronaald was already considered one of the men. He was fourteen years old, tall and strong with brown eyes and blond hair. Ronaald hunted seals and walrus; he fished for cod and haddock in the bay. There was even a robe made of the furs which Ronaald had brought home. Edith did nothing but watch her father's sheep and cattle, and help her mother to sew and tend the garden — these were her jobs. And all the while Ronaald was on wonderful adventures.

*　　*　　*

The next morning after breakfast Edith paused outside the cottage door and gazed longingly at the towering mountain peaks beyond the village.

Her powerful father had shivered when she coaxed him for a closer look. "You have heard the ice moan and roar," he said. "That should frighten you. Why do you ask and ask? You know you can't go and that I must say no. One must be very sharp-eyed and sure-footed to be safe on the peaks."

"Father, you say this but you let Ronaald go."

"Ronaald is nearly a man. You are only a very young

girl. I worry about Ronaald. How much more would I worry if I had to watch out for you too."

"Then leave him at home and take me."

Her father rubbed a big, work-worn hand over his sand-coloured beard. "You are a woman already with your coaxing! Well, no matter, you can't go. Not this year. Not next year. Perhaps the year after that."

The year after next was so far away. It might as well be never.

She trudged down to the meadow to watch over the sheep that grazed in the spring sunshine. Their pasture was between the stone and turf hut and the long fjord that stretched into the Atlantic. But while she was supposed to be minding the sheep, she was sitting on a rock — planning. Planning how she might be able to go on the village's next hunting trip.

She glanced at the streams of clear, cold water which ran down from the mountains and through the meadow. It would be lovely to go to their source. She had longed to see more wildlife ever since she watched a great polar bear floating by like a glowing spirit on an ice floe. The reindeer, hare and fox awaited.

"I will go," she said aloud. It did not matter to her that she would be travelling with a quarrelsome group of hunters. Father and Ronaald will be close by, she thought.

She jumped up in anger and flung a stone in the pond. The flat stone struck the water and it bounced once, twice, three times. "Stones cannot jump," she said. She had spoken aloud again and the sheep turned to her.

Rocks could not jump on water! She searched for more flat stones. All that afternoon she practised. Soon she could make the stones jump five and even six times.

For several days Edith was very happy. Children crowded around her to watch her new trick with the stones and learn how to make them skip.

One warm day Edith was happy to see her friend Margret coming slowly toward her. Margret had trouble walking. Of all my friends I feel happiest to see Margret, Edith mused as she greeted the other girl.

"Pick the flat ones and hold them just so," Edith said, skimming a rock over the pool.

It was not long before Margret mastered the game and they competed happily to see who could make their stones jump the farthest.

Anna and Kirsten Gunnarsdottir joined them. The sisters were strong and chose big rocks which they threw with ease far into the pool.

"It's the little flat ones that do well," Margret explained.

Anna and Kirsten were determined to succeed with the biggest rocks they could throw and were soon disappointed.

"Let's all swim," cried Anna. She stripped off her outer garments and was quickly joined by her sister in the sun-warmed water.

Trouble followed the girls' every escapade and Edith

watched nervously. Margret and I are right to keep our distance from them, Edith thought, for at times they can be unkind.

"Come on in, Edith," Kirsten shouted.

"I will keep Margret company," Edith replied.

Anna and Kirsten laughed at her as they splashed out into the deeper, colder water. "Skip me a stone," Anna called. "I'll catch it in my teeth."

"It would be better not to laugh," Margret advised Edith. "They know you are afraid of the deep water and they may pull you in."

The Gunnarsdottir sisters were easily distracted and forgetful of their chores, so it was not surprising to hear someone calling them home.

Edith's smile faded. "Skipping stones doesn't seem wonderful anymore," she told Margret. "One day I will do something truly amazing."

Chapter Two

"How can I make everyone respect me?" Edith asked herself over and over again. "How?"

"How what?" Ronaald asked. "I thought you were supposed to be watching sheep. I just drove one back from the cliff."

Edith shivered. She had forgotten the sheep. "Don't worry. I would have been there on time."

"You would?" Ronaald asked doubtfully.

"Why don't you stay and help me?"

"Father and I are going for a great piece of driftwood."

"Run along to the beach then, while your sister guards the mutton and wool."

Ronaald scowled at her. "You aren't very nice lately."

Edith was suddenly sorry for her unkind words.

"I suppose you still think you are going on the hunting trip, don't you?" Ronaald asked. "You're as silly as a lemming."

To Ronaald the little mice-like lemmings were the silliest creatures in the world. When the lemmings were short of food they gathered together and ran. If they didn't grow weary or find food they would run all the way to the ocean and drown.

The sea breeze had flushed Edith's heart-shaped face pink. Her eyes were very serious.

"Go ahead. Dream," Ronaald said. "I, too, have my dreams."

Edith followed her brother's eyes down to the ship that had been hauled up on the beach for repairs. The *Signe* was their settlement's one and only ship. It sailed to Iceland for supplies and to Markland for wood. Even Edith, who hated ships, admired the *Signe*. Soon twenty of the village's finest sailors would man the ship — men so big they looked like blond giants. The *Signe* would sail southward for wood.

Edith admired the long, heavy cargo ship for its sturdiness. The bow of the *Signe* differed from other ships. The bows of most vessels she had seen carried carvings of ugly monsters. Not so with the *Signe*. The wood carving was of the head and shoulders of a beautiful woman. The head was lifted proudly, the hair carved in a flying wing. Next to the lady, two wooden dragons were carved in detail. Every scale was scraped out of the wood and dyed reddish purple. A row of shields lined the sides of the ship. Though Edith had heard the settlers quarrel over the design Haakon had created for the ship, arguing that a fierce image was needed for protection, she felt those strong men were secretly proud of its difference. She wondered if it might already have shielded them on their voyages.

A tarpaulin for protection was located amidship, and there the supplies were stowed. The ship was more than fifty feet long and about fifteen feet wide. Edith knew that Ronaald was impressed and wished some day to be the commander.

"It isn't the right ship for you, Ronaald," Edith said, echoing what her mother had already told him.

Ronaald grinned. "Does the prow bother you? It is just Haakon's way to defy public opinion."

"Well that won't frighten enemies or sea monsters. I heard Gunnar tell Father that when the *Signe* meets disaster it will be because Haakon the Hateful must have everything his own stubborn way."

"Yet Gunnar still sails with him," Ronaald reasoned.

Edith pulled her eyes away from the ship and turned back toward the meadow with a toss of her hair. "Sailing ships isn't the only important thing," she said. "There must be something I can do to prove that I am as strong and brave as any man."

"But what can you do?" asked Ronaald.

When she heard sympathy in Ronaald's voice Edith was encouraged to say, "I have been thinking of a hunting trip on Walrusnose Mountain."

*   *   *

That evening there was much talk in the stone and sod hut. A party of men was soon going north to hunt. They would be away for weeks.

"Father," Edith said, trying to attract his attention.

"Be quiet," her mother cautioned. Edith's mother sounded short-tempered. As they worked together preparing supplies for the men's trip, she told Edith her own dream, "Like you, I would rather be on the hunt, but I must stay here and worry as I work."

"I understand," Edith said, for she knew that during the hunt she and her mother would worry together.

"It seems that if I were along, the hunting party wouldn't disappear," her mother said.

"And if it were lost for months or years," Edith said. "We would be there to help." She was filled with hope. Her mother did understand!

"And if we were in Norway . . ." her mother's fanciful mood continued. Edith had often heard those words and laughed.

"Don't trouble your father," her mother added softly. "He has many worries. Come and help me weave cloth. We will dye it bright colours and you shall have a new dress."

Edith went to her mother's side but she saw Ronaald looking at her.

"So spoiled," she heard him say.

"Don't be unkind," his father said.

"Perhaps I should pull a long face," Ronaald said. "I would rather go on the ship for wood than go hunting."

"Be content for now," his father said. "Fretting will not hasten your success."

*   *   *

Every day Hela, the old sheep, would come to Edith and Edith would pet Hela's head and rub her ears. There was no time to fuss with all the sheep, but Hela thought she was a special animal. And so she was.

Today Edith sat dreaming on a big rock in the pasture with Hela and the other sheep grazing nearby. The hunters were soon to leave on their trip north. It was not unheard of for girls to go on hunting trips. Perhaps this time she would follow the hunters. By the time they discovered her it would be too late to turn back.

Edith noticed that the sea wind had begun to blow very coldly. She got up to walk and keep warm. No one cares about me, she thought. Not even the sheep. She began looking for Hela. The flock ate contentedly, their black faces down to the thick grass — all the sheep but Hela.

Edith ran all over the field but she couldn't find Hela. "Hela! Hellie! Hellie!" she called.

She circled the pasture again, her swift young feet speeding over the rough ground. She dashed over to the stables, low buildings made of driftwood and stones and sod. Of course Hela had not gone in the stables on such a sunny day. Back Edith ran to the pasture, her voice growing shrill as she called over and over, "Hela! Where are you?"

Edith carefully counted the sheep. No matter how many times she counted, there were only nineteen. "How can I have lost her?" she said aloud. "Our best sheep! And just when I wanted Father pleased with me!"

Edith dragged her feet toward the cliff. It seemed she was not even able to watch sheep properly. Certainly she'd done nothing to impress her father, and now she must admit that she might never find her dearest sheep. She hardly dared look over the cliff. Hela might already be floating in the wild, cold water at the bottom of the fjord, and the waters of the fjord made Edith tremble.

Carefully Edith crept forward. She looked down at the deep water but couldn't see anything. There was nothing there but the roaring sea. The westerly wind blew strong and salty, tossing her hair back like a pale flag. She felt dizzy and eased away from the cliff edge. The wind howled against the jagged rocks and the gulls circled around her. And then she heard another sound.

There it was again. A soft 'baa-ahh'. Edith knelt and leaned over the cliff as far as she dared and looked straight down. Her heart pounded very hard.

There was Hela, standing on a ledge so narrow that she was pressed flat against the cliff.

"Edith!"

Edith jumped at the sound of her name. She turned and saw Margret walking slowly across the field toward her, aided by the stick her father had carved for her.

Edith put her finger to her lips. She was afraid Hela would move if she heard voices.

Margret lay down to look over the cliff edge. "What do you see?" she whispered.

Edith pulled her back. "Now don't you fall over too. Sit here while I think."

Margret sat back from the cliff edge.

"Hela is trapped on a ledge. At any minute she may topple into the water."

"Oh, poor Hela!" Margret reached for her stick. "I will go for help. Hela is my friend also. We will save the silly old thing."

Edith crawled to the cliff's edge as Margret made her way back across the field to the hut. Once again Edith's heart raced with fear. It would not be long before Hela tired or panicked. There was no time to waste.

The narrow ledge below her ran along the face of the cliff leading to a corner of the pasture. It might be possible to coax Hela along the ledge, yet the poor sheep looked too frightened to walk anywhere. Even from where Edith lay she could see the sheep trembling. Without someone to lead her, she would surely fall. Without a hand to guide her, Hela would likely never see the pasture again. "If I am to save her," Edith whispered, "I must not look down at the sea."

There was no choice. Edith's father and the other

men were in a far hayfield today. By the time they came it would be too late.

Not daring to look down even once, Edith made her move. She slipped her feet over the edge of the cliff and felt for toe holds. How thankful she was for going barefoot in the summer, for her feet were hard. It was also easier for her bare toes to find a hold than it would be if she wore shoes.

Her toes were able to feel the small cracks in the rocks. These cracks became Edith's stairway. Slowly, slowly, she inched down the cliff.

The wind was hard against her back. It was like a hand helping to steady her against the rock face.

Then for one terrible moment her feet slipped, swinging free while only her finger tips gripped a small handhold. After what seemed like an eternity, one of Edith's feet found a narrow crack in the rock. As she pushed her toes into the crack, a rock was knocked loose. It bounced down the cliff before splashing into the water far below.

At last, one of her feet touched the wool on Hela's back. The wool was cooled by the breeze and felt soft against her foot. She moved a little and lowered herself onto the ledge so she was standing in front of Hela. Her hands and feet were trembling and filthy from the climb. Seeing her friend, Hela stopped trembling and nuzzled Edith's hand with her moist nose.

Edith had no time to fuss over her bleeding hands and feet. Her rescue plan had brought her safely to the friendly sheep's side. But now she noticed just how narrow the ledge was. She was filled with dread of what awaited her below if she made one wrong move. She shook off the feeling of water closing in over her head.

"We won't think of it, Hela," she whispered soothingly, "No, we won't think of it."

Chapter Three

"Hellie, Hellie, come with me. Come slowly with me." Edith talked softly to Hela, afraid that at any moment the old sheep might stumble and fall. With her hand on Hela's head she coaxed her carefully along the edge of the dangerous precipice.

Hela's large eyes were on Edith as the girl gently talked her along the ledge. Hela's thin old legs quivered as she took cautious step after cautious step, obediently moving only when Edith told her to, her frightened eyes on her mistress. The only sound Edith could hear was her own voice.

Backward along the narrow ledge she worked her way, her hand under the sheep's chin. Finally, when Edith thought her strength was surely gone, they reached the lip of the pasture. She scrambled over the bank and onto the grass, but it was too high for Hela.

"Oh what shall I do," Edith thought out loud. She dared not go for help, for Hela might become confused and fall.

She coaxed, and the animal tried her best but it was hopeless. "Come on, Hela, try. Oh please try to get up, just once more."

"Here!" Suddenly her father was beside her, lifting the sheep up off the ledge in his powerful arms and setting her on the grass. Edith flung her arms about the sheep. "We are safe," she cried. "Father, how did you come here?"

"Margret came to the far field. I ran down here and I saw you weren't in sight. I was afraid and I looked over the cliff. Just as I looked, I saw your head disappearing along the ledge. I ran down here but I didn't dare speak for fear of startling you. You shouldn't have risked your life for a sheep."

"She isn't just a sheep, Father. Margret says, 'Hela is everyone's friend'. She is the friendliest of all the animals. Often when I am lonely, I talk to her."

"It was a brave and wonderful thing you did, Edith. The risk was great. I don't know anyone else in the settlement who would have dared. Nor do I know anyone else who, daring, would have succeeded."

All the way back up to the stable with the sheep he kept looking at his daughter and murmuring. "A brave and wonderful thing! So very brave."

That evening Edith went to her father with a happy smile. "Father, do you wish me to get ready?"

"Ready?"

"Ready to go north."

He laughed. "Ah, Edith. Won't you forget the idea?"

"It was you who said I was brave, Father."

"You are only a child," he replied. "I will hear no more about this."

"I am the bravest in all the settlement, Father. I did something not even the men could do. You said this yourself. Surely now I have proven myself and may go with you tomorrow."

Her father's voice became more impatient. "Wasn't Margret also brave to come to the field for me? There was no one at the hut so she came with only her stick to help her. It must have been very painful for her, and yet she doesn't ask for praise or favours. I will not have you go on a dangerous and tiring trip that you know nothing about. Can you handle a bone harpoon or a spear? You couldn't carry supplies, you are too small. I will be forced to become very angry if I hear any more of this foolish plan of yours. Your place is with your mother, and here you stay."

Edith tossed her head angrily but her lips quivered. That night in bed, she began to cry. It just wasn't fair. Father had admitted she was brave. She had searched for a way to show him how brave she was and it hadn't helped. There was to be no reward for her deed. Bitterly she wept far into the night.

When morning came Edith woke and dressed. Her mother was by the fire heating milk. "I steamed fish for the men and now we will breakfast together."

"They are gone then, gone North without me," Edith said, and the tears rolled down her cheeks.

"Yes, they are gone."

"I don't wish to eat breakfast."

Her mother did not insist, "I am fixing a warm milk drink for you. Then you will lie down and sleep. I know you slept very little during the night. It is early yet."

"Yes, Mother," Edith said. She was so downcast she did not give any thought to the fine powder of herbs that her mother added to the milk, a mixture of nerve root that would help bring on sleep. Edith could barely control her tears. Yesterday had been a very trying day.

"What you need is a nice, dreamless sleep, then you will be able to look on things with more reason," her mother told her.

Edith was grateful for the warm milk. "I think that I will lie down now," she said as she sipped the last of the milk. But the moment her mother went to tend the livestock she got up and stood in the doorway. She felt too restless to lie down just yet. The softness of the fresh air drew her outside.

Birds were singing and the air was strong with salt from the breeze blowing in from the sea. It was a cool and quiet day and Edith began to walk along the shore of the fjord. She walked until she was in sight of the ship, the *Signe*. It was anchored in the harbour where it sat prepared for its trip south for timber. The calming effect of the herbs made her feel that her unhappiness was selfish and silly. Things could not always be the way people wanted them, after all. Ronaald had wanted to be on the ship and now he was on the hunt.

She loved their beautiful country at this time of year. The sun glinting on the tips of the ice-capped mountains turned them an icy green that matched the hue of the glaciers. With the blue-green of the pastures it made a delightful picture.

Why do people leave? Edith asked herself. People were never content. Maybe it was the long closed-in winters. People were always leaving. They were always off to Iceland. Or Ireland. Or Norway. Or even to explore in Markland.

She sat down and rested against a big stone. It was difficult to remember why she was here. Shouldn't she be tending the sheep? The landscape looked strange and she didn't know which path she had taken.

Perhaps if she were to sleep a little . . .

The sound of laughter made Edith raise her head. There were Anna and Kirsten Gunnarsdottir, smiling down at her.

"Are you really sleeping, lazy Edith?" Anna teased. "You should be on the cliff face tending your sheep."

Edith thought this was funny but she was too tired to laugh. "What was my mother saying about sleep?" she asked. "Do help me, girls," she mumbled. "I want to go home."

"Of course," Anna said. Edith felt very small as Anna and Kirsten took her elbows and easily guided her along with their strong, young arms.

Edith tried to concentrate on what her friends were talking and laughing about, but nothing seemed clear except the firm grip they had on her arms. She let them guide her on and on. Edith fell against Anna and straightened up only to fall against Kirsten, and then they helped her onto her bed. She felt the fur robe under her and wanted to thank the girls but words wouldn't come to her.

"Wait until she wakes!" exclaimed Kirsten, still laughing.

"Let's sit here until she does," Edith heard Anna say.

Why don't they go home? Edith wondered sleepily.

In a little while she heard the voice of Anna and Kirsten's elder sister calling and scolding, then Edith heard nothing more. Her last feeling was of being gently rocked as she breathed soft, salty air.

*   *   *

Edith's mother worked about the farmyard. She thought of her husband and her son on their way north. I wish I could have gone with them, she thought. I would be of use on such a trip. Still it is my job to stay at home and keep the farm going. I'll not worry about the hunters, but put aside thoughts of the great ice sheets cracking and sliding. She had to believe the men who set out with bows and arrows and spears would return with game and tales of adventure.

She loved the summer, but in the winter her family

was near to home. They went hunting for seal and walrus, but these were close by. The ice was solid then, and did not shift like a mighty trap waiting for someone to walk on it.

No more sad thoughts, the mother told herself. I will think of Edith, my very fair-haired daughter, asleep in the hut. Tonight when the chores are finished I will go in and wake the child from her deep sleep. We will have each other for company and be busy so the days will go quickly.

The mother stood at the top of the green pasture. With her hand on the stone fence she gazed over the fjord, looking along the stretch of water. The clear blue sky seemed to blend right into the grey blue of the ocean. She could see the sail of the ship, setting off on the voyage to Markland for timber.

She turned back to her tasks. There is much to do but tomorrow Edith will help, she thought. For today, let the child rest.

It was late evening before she completed her chores and returned to find she was alone in the hut.

Chapter Four

Edith woke with a start. She lay in the dark for a moment listening. Great cracking sounds filled the air. It was a sound she had often heard — the noise of ice breaking. A moment later she heard the monstrous splash of the ice sliding off a cliff into the sea. It was as if a mountain had toppled into the ocean. She stirred a little and tried to sleep again.

She heard another sound she did not understand. It was a brisk, snapping sound, like something flying in the wind. She sat up and listened. It was then that she heard the sound of water and realized she was under a tarpaulin and on a boat. Her heart thumped with fear.

I must get up right now and go home, she thought. Mother is alone and will be worried, and there is work to catch up on. How did I come to be here? Mother will be searching all over for me.

She could hear the sound of the sail slapping in the wind and the sound of footfall and voices. Men were on the ship.

She leaned back on the bundle of furs and her skin

felt cold with fear. She must have been asleep for hours. The ship had sailed and she was on it and it would go down the coast of Helluland with her on board.

The last I remember, Anna and Kirsten were bringing me home and they were laughing, she thought. How can I be on a ship?

The realization of what must have happened made her feel ill. They thought I'd wake up and see the water and it would be a joke. "But I didn't wake up," she gasped. "And they were called away. Oh! Someone must help me get home."

Who were the men sailing this ship? She pictured grim, unsmiling sailors. How could she make them understand that she had boarded their ship by accident? Everyone knew the ship was to go out for wood. She could only expect them to be angry.

She had never wanted to go sailing. Yesterday during her climb on the cliff it had not been the height that had kept her from looking down, but the sea below. Last summer when she had been out in her father's small fishing boat it had made them both ill.

Perhaps the sailors would regard her as a nuisance and fling her into the ocean. It might be wise to creep in among the supplies surrounding her and remain hidden. She prayed that the sea would stay smooth and she would not be ill.

Terrified, she crouched in a dark corner under the ill-smelling tarpaulin. The ship swayed as it raced along, making the best possible use of the wind. Now and then she would hear a shout and the thud of running feet.

It was late now. She heard movement near her and then a sailor came close enough to be seen from her hideaway. The man said, "That's a good wind, Erik."

Edith recognized this sailor. He was *Haakon the Hateful*. Of course he was not called *the Hateful* to his face, but Haakon had earned the name. He was tall, strong-looking, and very heavy. His hair was darker than the average Greenlander's and he was very handsome. He knew the ways of the north. Edith remembered hearing much about Haakon. It was said that one of his parents belonged to the Thule, the people from the north who hunted and fished in light skin boats. It was also said that he had learned many of their skills, but he had not learned their peaceful ways. He had married the beautiful Signe, for whom the ship was named. She was tall and strong and had lovely hair and a pretty face. Why she married Haakon, no one could guess. Some thought that in a land of mostly blond men, she may have found his dark hair very handsome. Certainly she did not seem at all like her fierce husband.

Haakon started almost every quarrel in the settlement. He was usually accusing someone of stealing from him. Many of these quarrels ended in fights in which Haakon would beat his enemy. This was why he had earned the name, *Haakon the Hateful*.

"Yes it is a good wind," Erik answered. "It would be

a shame to waste it. I haven't seen much ice either. We are making wonderful time."

"All this effort just for timber," said Haakon with a sneer.

"Perhaps we will find something else."

"In Markland? Low hills and trees, that is all we will see. If all they want is timber," Haakon said, "Why don't the fools move to Markland? There are said to be wondrous lands south of here. Why should we stay in that miserable Greenland when there are better things waiting for us?"

Erik did not answer and in a moment Haakon went on. "There's a land where one can reach out and clutch great handfuls of grapes from the vines; where things grow without being cultivated. There is a land that is always summer. A land without ice and snow."

"Strange and dangerous dragons are said to be there," Erik said. "And we know nothing of the people."

"We can handle whatever comes. Besides, why would we leave the best part of this new land to others?" Haakon asked.

Edith knew nothing of the people to the south. The unknown was so terrifying that even this dreadful ship suddenly seemed like a haven. At least it can take me home, she thought.

Erik's voice grew quiet. "The seas are said to be so hot that they boil. There are said to be dragons and snakes that rise out of the water and spit fire."

Haakon gave a hard laugh. "How much like a child

or a woman you are. Are you not a man? Must you always find fears where there is nothing to be afraid of? I have talked to men who have sailed to the south of France. It is like a paradise where all men live with the riches of kings. Who is to say there isn't something as wonderful south of Greenland?"

Edith was terribly uncomfortable crouched in her hiding place. She felt ill and hungry and thirsty all at once. The men moved as if to leave, and now she could only see their feet. They lingered, talking of the people they called the *Shore-ones* who lived on the coast south of Greenland. Haakon complained that he had been unable to trade his furs. The Greenlanders and the Shore-ones both had furs to trade, and they all wanted silks, coloured clothes, ornaments, knives and cooking pots.

Finally Edith heard Erik say, "Let's go and sleep. It will soon be our watch."

The two moved away and Edith sighed with relief. She was safe, at least for a little while. The talk of going south frightened her. She thought they were going to Markland for timber. Many years ago Norsemen had built settlements on Markland and even further south in a place called Vineland. Edith had heard these settlements were no more and wondered what had driven the people from their homes.

All this was too much for Edith. Her fears mounted up like the stone fence at home onto which every passerby placed another rock. She felt as if those fears were being piled on her chest, making it difficult for her to breathe under the weight.

There were things she could not help imagining. First she saw her mother's fear, and then her mother's loneliness and sorrow. She imagined her father's return, and his rage and heartbreak. Ronaald would be lonely, for he would no longer have a sister. Even the sheep would miss her when she was not there to tend them. Hela would look for her, as she herself had looked for Hela. And her friends would miss her too, Anna and Kirsten and most of all Margret.

I must decide what to do, Edith thought. We will be gone for two weeks or more and I will need food and water. The ship is too small for me to remain hidden and the sea will make me ill, even if there is no storm. I might as well show myself now.

As she crept forward to come out of hiding, she saw that a skin container Haakon had been drinking from was left at the side of the tarpaulin. Perhaps this was a sign telling her to remain hidden. The sea was calm and it was growing dark as she drew the container under her shelter. There was only a small quantity of water but it relieved her thirst and she dozed off.

When she woke again she felt ill, too ill to think of eating. She was also very thirsty. The ship rocked and tossed and no one came near her. That could mean all hands were needed to take in the heavy sail. The darkness and the toss of the ship and the shouts and running feet were frightening. Miserable and seasick, she longed for her mother and the comfort her mother could give. There was a herb in one of the skin bags in their house that could help her now. It would soothe her aching stomach.

"We are sure to capsize," she moaned. "We will crash into an iceberg or the rocks."

The ship rocked and tossed and creaked in the fierce storm. She heard the sail tear with a great ripping sound. Then came the sound of the sail flapping wildly in the storm. The wild ride continued until daylight.

"Has it ended?" she finally asked. The boat still rocked but the roar of the wind was gone and with it the dreadful snap of the torn sail. The cursing and shouting of the men had changed to joking and loud laughter.

Edith noticed a woman preparing a meal in the dull light of early morning. The woman had long hair of spun gold and was very beautiful. This must be Signe, the wife of Haakon the Hateful. Edith was so glad to see a woman on the ship that she almost spoke. One thing kept her quiet — the woman was the wife of the evil Haakon. After a few minutes the woman picked up the food she had prepared for the sailors and disappeared from Edith's sight.

Edith crept to where Signe had opened the bag of dried food and helped herself. Her stomach was still sore from her seasickness, but she felt much better after she ate a little of the meat. Then she searched for the water barrels but they were nowhere to be seen. They must be stored on the open deck. She sat down feeling as if she would cry. Her thirst had been great, but after eating the dry food it was even worse.

The more she thought of coming out of hiding, the more afraid she became. She knew if she waited longer her courage would be gone. She must have something to drink, just a little water. Already she was nearly wild with thirst. Quickly, before she could change her mind, she left her hiding place and stood, wavering unsteadily on the deck.

Chapter Five

A rolling fog hid the terrifying sea from Edith. She staggered a little as the ship rolled gently, and she trembled as she looked at the men eating their meal. How strange their faces looked through the fog.

A soft breeze blew grey mist between Edith and the dreaded sailors. It was Haakon who noticed Edith standing there.

"Am I to believe my eyes?" he sputtered in amazement. "The Thule told me . . . warned me . . ."

The startled sailors looked up from their food. What is happening? Edith wondered. Instead of being angry they seemed afraid. She tried to smile at Signe, but her dry lips did little more than tremble.

"She is of the Spirit World," Haakon said and he turned nervously to the carving of the woman's head on the ship's prow.

"You babies!" said Signe with a laugh. "This spirit is but a little stowaway, and I believe she is ill."

One man cried out, "It's my little girl. It is my poor dead little girl."

"No, it isn't," Edith said. "It's only me and I'd like a drink of water."

"Are you certain, Bjorn?" exclaimed another.

"My little Fjola fell into a rushing stream ten years ago and drowned," the man replied, gazing at Edith. "You are her spirit, are you not?"

"No. I am Edith Valgardsdottir. I fell asleep on your ship and here I am. Oh, please, I would like a drink of water."

There was a long pause while the fog drifted about the silent group, hiding from Edith any friendly expression there may have been on the solemn faces. Haakon was the first to recover. "Throw her overboard. She is the one who has brought us bad luck. She brought the storm and caused us to drift we know not where. She brought the fog," he roared. "Throw her overboard."

One man with a thin and hard face got up with a growl of agreement, but Bjorn took his arm. "Stay, Olaf!"

Signe stepped forward. "Don't be such an awful windbag," she said to Haakon. She handed Edith a bowl of water and put her hand on the girl's shoulder.

"She is an evil spirit, I tell you," Haakon insisted.

"Oh nonsense!" Signe said. She turned back to Edith. "There, dear. Are you feeling better?"

"Yes, thank you," Edith said in a small voice.

She saw the thin-faced man, Olaf, the one who had been ready to throw her overboard. "Perhaps she is a spirit," he said. "It is quite a thing to have such a bad storm come up so quickly, and now we have this dense fog. If she brought these things, she must have powers."

"Then we will use her powers to find land and get us out of this mist safely," Signe replied.

"Please believe me," Edith said. "I am just an ordinary girl. You must have seen me on my father's farm. We are not rich, but if you do not throw me overboard my father will give you what he can."

"I think we will discuss this," Haakon said. He motioned for the thin man to come with him a little way from the others. "Come, Olaf."

Edith shivered as the two men whispered together. She looked over at Signe. "Will they kill me?"

"No, of course they won't." She put her lips close to Edith's ear. "Trust me."

Haakon returned with the evil-faced Olaf. "We have decided to keep her alive. If she can lead us out of the fog, she will be safe, but if she can't . . ." He made a tossing motion to the side of the ship.

A young man not much older than Ronaald stepped forward. "Come on now, Haakon." It was Erik — Edith knew his voice from hearing him speak with Haakon about the boiling sea and dragons. "It isn't the little girl's fault we had storms, and there must be some reason why she is on the ship. I don't imagine she wants to be here."

"I thought we agreed that Olaf and I would organize this trip. We are the most experienced," Haakon said.

Erik did not look at the fierce Haakon as he asked, "Is it reasonable to make such a fuss over a child?"

Haakon stepped forward as if to strike Erik but Signe put her hand on his arm. "Stay, Haakon. We need to stand together to sail the ship."

"This is true, Signe," Haakon sneered. "This is true. Now Erik, remember, your sister had to speak for you."

Erik did not answer and Edith could see little of his face in the fog. All the while she searched for the faces of her father's friends, Gunnar, and the older man, Larus. Why couldn't she see them? She had heard Gunnar tell her father that he and Larus would be sailing with Haakon.

The day passed. They sailed on and on in the calm and fogbound seas, and they knew not where.

The fog chilled Edith but she did not want to go under the wool tarpaulin.

She knew from the talk around her that they had lost their way in the storm with neither sun nor stars to guide them.

Some of the tired seamen were working on the torn sail, while others were ready at the oars. When the fog lifted a little, Edith could see the men staring at her as she searched for the faces of Gunnar and Larus, or anyone else who might know she was Edith Valgardsdottir.

These strong men, with drops of mist clinging to their beards, looked alike to her tired eyes. Now and then someone would call loudly, "Do you hear that?"

The men grew quarrelsome. Signe was the only one who looked calm as she waited, ready to take an oar if needed. Edith sat on a coil of rope and thought the strong and beautiful Signe would make a splendid queen for any country, but King Haakon would not do.

"What are they listening for?" Edith asked.

"We are afraid of crashing and capsizing," Signe said. "They are listening for the lashing sounds of the sea on the coast rocks or an iceberg."

"Are you afraid?"

Signe smiled sweetly, "No. I have learned not to be afraid. I have been married for many years to a very brave man."

Edith's eyes were big with surprise, for she thought Signe was too clever to be proud of such a mean husband.

"I know you are thinking he is a cruel man, but he is also brave and hardworking."

Edith thought she would rather be on a ship where all the sailors were lazy and afraid, if only they were kind.

All the men are nervous except Haakon, Edith thought. What can his good mood mean?

"I think we are going south," Haakon said, looking satisfied. "Soon we will drift to the new land. It is always summer there, with so much wild game and fruit no one need ever work."

The round-faced Erik said, "I hope you are right, but I am cold. It feels more as if we are drifting north."

"Afraid are you?" Haakon said with his usual contempt. "Are you afraid of sea monsters and snakes that spit fire? We are going south, Erik. Tell me if the ocean is on fire."

Erik moved back to the sail-mending and Olaf took his place. Olaf was very thin but his arms rippled with muscles. His mouth looked as if it had never turned upwards in all his life. He spoke to Haakon but pointed at Edith. "How long will we let the evil one live? She has done nothing to take away the fog. Surely our bad luck would leave us if we were to throw her into the ocean."

"I will decide if our luck is good or bad," Haakon said and glanced at Signe. Although he wasn't afraid of the nineteen men on the boat, it seemed to Edith he might be just a little afraid of Signe. "She brought us through the storm and now we are drifting toward Vineland. Wouldn't you rather sunbathe in Vineland than cut wood in Markland?"

"I will give her three days," Olaf said. "If the fog is not gone three days from now, I will see she has a taste of salt water."

"In three days we may all be dead," growled another man, and others agreed.

"She is only a child," Bjorn said. "Like my daughter was."

"We must use her powers to help us," Haakon said.

"You are all talking silly," Erik called from his new place on one of the benches. "How can grown men believe a child is a spirit? She can do us no harm. Why must you frighten her with your threats?"

"If she is a spirit," Olaf said, "She won't sink when we throw her overboard."

"Perhaps we can feed her to one of Erik's sea monsters," Haakon said, laughing at his own joke.

"Come near," Erik called, and Edith approached him at the oars and sat on the bench. The sea was frighteningly close. "Don't be afraid," Erik told her quietly. "I am Signe's younger brother. Haakon enjoys making fun of me." He added bitterly, "I wish I had not been persuaded to come."

When Edith looked hard at Erik, she could see he looked a little like his sister. But he was not calm as was Signe. Again she noticed how young he was. Talking to him increased her longing for Ronaald and home.

"I don't like those bullies being the navigators," Erik said. "We made a mistake choosing Olaf and Haakon. It has divided the crew and will weaken us in times of danger."

"You worry too much," said Signe who had been nearby listening.

"But Signe, you know Gunnar is a good navigator and Larus is even better, for he studies much."

"Are Larus and Gunnar on board?" Edith asked, rising unsteadily to her feet. "How wonderful . . ."

"They are in the aft," Erik told her. "Gunnar had a fall in the storm and can't be moved. Larus is trying to revive him." Erik's face became thoughtful. "We are shorthanded. You are very small but you could help us. Perhaps then Haakon . . ."

"Oh, Erik," Edith interrupted. "Take me to them. Gunnar knows me well and even Larus may recognize me." Her courage had returned and she wobbled toward the rear of the ship. Erik started to follow but a sudden warning shout sent him hurrying to the oars.

Edith could hear the crashing of water against something and she toppled to the deck as the craft rolled. With a mighty effort the oarsmen pulled to move the ship away from danger. Edith glimpsed a towering wall of ice alongside the ship. She put her hands over her eyes. "The sea! The sea!" she moaned, expecting to feel it close over her at any moment.

As it had been with the storm in the night, she was suddenly aware that the shouting had stopped, the pounding waves were silent, and though they had all been drenched with water, she now heard the men laughing. Bjorn and another sailor left the oars and joked as they bailed water from the centre of the ship.

How quickly the sailors recover from these emergencies, she thought, while I scarcely remember what I was doing before our fright!

The excitement almost made Edith forget Gunnar and Larus. She moved unsteadily to the stern where it was now very wet. Larus was lifting a wool tarpaulin that had protected a silent figure sprawled in a dim triangle formed by the end of the ship.

"Larus," she said faintly, for she had always been afraid of his stern face. "Do you know me? I am Edith Valgardsdottir."

The old man looked up. His grey hair was wet and matted on his scowling brow. "What are you doing on this ship, child?"

Edith's hopes died when she heard him say *child* with a tone usually saved for words such as *vermin*. She managed a reply. "It was by accident. Please, don't you know me?" By now she was struggling with tears and was shamed when she felt one roll down her cheek.

"Who did you say your father is?" Larus asked.

"Valgard," Edith said.

"Yes, I know the farmer Valgard and his boy, Ronaald, And who are you?"

Once again she told him but he seemed to have little thought for anything other than the care of Gunnar.

"I don't remember you," he said.

Edith knelt on the other side of the unconscious man. There was enough light in the triangle where he lay for Edith to see it was indeed Gunnar, the good-natured father of Anna and Kirsten. His face was ashen and his ragged breathing made Edith forget the groans of the ship and the hiss of water by the stern. Though he had neither grey hair nor a lined face, Gunnar looked older than Larus. Would he die, she wondered, and be dropped into the sea or buried on the shores of Markland? Oh, his poor family! And poor me, Edith thought, what am I to do? She wrapped her arms about herself for comfort, for her hope of proving she was Edith Valgardsdottir was gone.

Edith stayed near Gunnar. From time to time, Larus

would leave the oars to raise his friend into a sitting position and force a little water between his lips.

"He is not looking any better," she would tell Larus, and he would nod and give her some small chore to help him. Gladly she fetched water or robes and helped mix the herbs Larus was bathing Gunnar's brow with.

She jumped when she heard Haakon's voice grumble to Larus about wasting water. "If the spirit doesn't lift the fog, we won't be able to go ashore for water."

Edith hurried away. Both Haakon and Olaf had insisted she should cure Gunnar as well as lift the fog. She sat by Signe where she felt safe.

As two days slowly crept by, Erik urged Edith to do more chores to win favour with the sailors. "I wish to clean and to bail, but I am so weak," she said. Erik brought her some of the powders Bjorn carried in case of seasickness but they didn't help. Lying on her side in the middle of the boat brought her some relief, though Haakon would jab her with his foot when he passed by.

As it grew dark Signe brought her another robe and said, "You will get better. It is just taking you time to get used to the sea."

As she drifted off to sleep Edith thought, how little time is left, the fog has held two days and two nights since Olaf's threat.

On the third morning Edith's first thought on waking was, will they really let Olaf throw me into the sea? Even as she framed the thought, a feeling close to happiness came over her. Her sickness was gone! She sat up and felt the sun on her face and realized she could now see from prow to stern. She even saw the carving of the woman's head and shoulders on the prow against a calm sea and blue sky.

A breeze blew away the last wisps of fog and the sun made its first appearance since the storm. By then no one knew what to expect. They were surrounded by a calm sparkling sea with neither floating ice nor debris of any kind. The sailors all smiled at Edith. She was not sure why they smiled, but could it be that they believed she had lifted the fog? Perhaps they were just glad Olaf would not throw her into the sea. Olaf had a very strong will. If he said, "I will throw you in the sea," it seemed to Edith that he meant it.

"This isn't the north anyway," Erik said. "It has turned very warm."

It was indeed warm. It was the warmest day Edith had known in all her life.

"We must be going south," Signe said.

"We are," Olaf agreed. "We know that by the sun."

"Is there anyone who does not wish to go south?" Haakon asked.

"We haven't enough food to take us home," a sailor said. "Why not find us your Vineland, Haakon? We will get more supplies."

Signe stood beside Edith. Edith noticed that Signe's hair was the colour of the primrose that grew among the rocks at home. A wave of homesickness swept over her.

Erik came and stood on the other side of his sister.

"Must we hold this course, Erik?" Signe asked.

"Unless it comes to mutiny," her brother replied. "We did vote Haakon and Olaf as leaders. Although the men are afraid of going hungry, they are excited. The sea is very calm and the air is so warm and lovely that they dream of Vineland."

"And what of Edith?" Signe asked. "She is to be separated from her family."

"It is the same for the sailors."

"They are used to it. They are men who have sought adventure."

Erik sighed. "It can't be helped. We have been away a week now and Edith's family has already suffered heartbreak. If she is ever to return, it will be a joyous day for them."

Edith shivered. Erik and Signe were speaking as if they might never return to Greenland. Just then Haakon joined them, putting his rough, soiled hand on her shoulder.

"You will find us land," he ordered in a low voice.

Edith drew away. Does he still think I have powers, she wondered, or is he just pretending for some reason of his own?

Signe heard him and said, "She lifted the fog. That should be more than enough for our little *just pretend spirit.*"

"Not quite enough," Haakon said crossly, and Edith was more afraid of him than ever. He was surely planning to use her in some scheme.

Edith wondered if Haakon had ever intended to return to Greenland. If Haakon and Olaf were as smart as everyone said they were, then they were not lost. They were sailing just where they wanted to sail.

The evening was warm. Edith settled on the fur rug Signe had given her and was soon asleep and dreaming of home. It was winter and her family was at home playing chess by the light of the seal oil lamp. It was a lovely dream.

She woke to the warm sun and the excited voices of the crew. The ship was moving slowly ahead, tossing a little on the gentle sea. Edith stood up and looked around, feeling as if she were in another dream. They were in a very large bay within a half circle of land and rolling hills. There were more trees and green plants than Edith had ever believed there could be.

"Vineland!" She whispered to herself. "We have arrived in Vineland."

Chapter Six

Edith gazed at the rolling green hills surrounding them. "Is this Markland or Helluland?" She asked Signe.

Signe looked surprised, as if she had forgotten Edith in her excitement. "I do not know where we are," she said. "All I know is that it is a new land. A beautiful land."

All around her the sailors were acting like children at a picnic. They cheered and laughed and sang as they neared the shoreline. The ship was moving toward what looked like a sandy beach.

Edith was afraid. The trees and hills were every bit as pretty as any story of Norway, yet she was afraid. This strange land could harm them, or delay their return to Greenland.

There was no wind and Erik was among the men using the oars. Edith could see his happy face and thought he had forgotten his fears of fire-breathing dragons. Good, she thought, for that belief was very silly. Even I haven't believed in such monsters for years!

Signe's eyes were shining and there was a wide smile

on her face. "What a lovely home we could build here," Signe said to Haakon.

"We will be rich and powerful," Haakon gloated, rubbing his hands together. "This is our land. Here I will be the king."

The sailors cheered Haakon, even Erik, who seemed to have forgotten how his brother-in-law treated him. Edith thought they acted as if Haakon the Hateful was already king of the land. Only Olaf did not cheer but stood glaring at Haakon.

Olaf then turned his attention to Edith. His face was like a skeleton and his eyes were like sharp blue beads. "You drove the fog away," he said. His lips twisted strangely as he tried to force his mouth into a smile.

Edith shook her head. She would like to tell Olaf that he was silly, but she couldn't because she was too afraid of him.

"You brought us to land," Olaf muttered. "You helped us and now I will help you." Olaf had the reputation of being a good navigator and a clever mathematician, yet in other ways she did not think him very smart.

Again Edith shook her head. She could see Olaf wanted her to admit to magic powers, but why? She backed into the stern, trying to escape him.

"Don't be afraid of me," he said. Again he tried to smile. His whole head seemed to shift and groan like a ship in a storm, his face twisting as he turned his lips up.

"With your power we can rule the new land," he said

in a low voice. "We do not need a *King Haakon*. You will be queen and I will advise you."

With an effort Edith gasped, "No! I only wish to return to Greenland. To go back to my parents and friends."

"You will only use your magical power when I tell you," Olaf said gruffly.

"I tell you I cannot do magic. If I could, I'd go home."

Just then the sailor, Ivar, called out to Olaf. "Come take an oar. It is not yet time to rest."

"Why are you teasing Edith, Olaf?" Erik joined in. "Why are you not singing with the rest of us? Do you not see the countryside that grows more lovely as we near it?" He laughed. "Do you see a little pasture the size of a handkerchief? Of course not. Here there are fields that stretch as far as the eye can see. You see rolling hills and lush forests."

Olaf snorted. "One hill. One bay. One field. One of each thing and you cheer. I would never be such a fool."

A low moan startled Edith. She stooped and looked into the space where Gunnar was. He was sitting up, his eyes rolling wildly.

"Larus," she screamed, but by the time Larus left the oars and joined them, Gunnar was once again on his back, his breathing slow and loud as it had been since his accident.

Larus raised Gunnar a little and tried to give him a vile-looking mixture of herbs and water. Much of the liquid spilled and Larus turned on Olaf angrily, "Get away from us, will you!"

Olaf looked at Gunnar with a satisfied expression. His dreadful smile was for Edith. "You will surely cure your friend. Did you not compel him to sit up and he did?"

Edith stared at him in wonder. He really does believe in magic, she thought.

Larus' voice was weary and impatient. "Get away from us, Olaf. Go elsewhere with your magic and spells."

Olaf urged Edith. "Won't you show your powers again and bring Gunnar back?"

Edith moved close to Larus and gazed down at Gunnar. Tears ran down her face as she thought, oh Gunnar, if I could cure you, I would. Then I would make Olaf disappear at the same time.

Olaf sat on a sack of supplies and mumbled to himself. Around him voices were raised in an old Norse song.

They camped that night on a stretch of beach below the barefaced rocks. Except for the tide, the ocean was quiet and smooth. Edith was glad to sleep on the beach with only her rug as a blanket, away from the boat where she had known so much fear and illness. Some of the sailors loved the boat so much they went back to sleep on it. Haakon sent Olaf with them to listen to anything they might say.

Edith heard Haakon tell Signe, "If anyone else plans

to be king, I want to know about it."

"Oh, do not trust Olaf," Signe replied. "He is filled with thoughts of power. It is clouding his mind."

Edith heard murmurings among the sailors over the next few days. Those who had families in Greenland wanted to cut timber and return home. The one named Jon suggested they take the boat back for their loved ones. Others didn't wish to do anything but sit on the beach and eat clams. They feared that if they left this land, they would never find it again.

One night as Edith settled for sleep, she heard Signe say to Haakon, "The sailors have been talking against you. They think you were never lost in the fog, that you should have told them this was your destination so they could come as pioneers."

Haakon laughed. "Let them build a ship and go home. I have not tied their hands."

"Think of them, Haakon," she implored. "A seaworthy boat does not build itself overnight."

"I am a clever man," Haakon boasted, rubbing a big hand over his beard. "Behold! I am King Haakon. I am *King Haakon the First of Plateauland*. As of this day I name this land, *Plateauland*."

Edith was only surprised he had not called it *Haakonland*.

Signe said, "Well I hope the sailors do not decide to hang their new king."

"What a strange jest, Signe," Haakon replied. "I have the loyalty of the sailors and we have the powers of the little girl on our side."

"You don't believe in that," Signe said.

"Of course not, but it would be easy to make the others believe."

Edith kept very still under her robe, so they would not know she listened.

Signe said, "Poor little Edith Valgardsdottir; daughter of a hunter and sheep farmer. How she must long for her busy, comfortable home."

"Never mind," Haakon said. "If she can't cast spells, she will still be useful. Since I am king and you are queen, you will need a servant."

In the morning there was an early fog such as those that often come by the ocean. Edith could see their ship anchored firmly on the beach, looking unreal in the drifting fog. At home the ship seemed huge, she thought, but it is a very small craft when on the wild sea.

As the sun rose they could see that the hills to their east were lined with white and red minerals, and mist lingered on the hilltops.

"Shall we build a house here?" Signe asked as she prepared a breakfast of fresh fish cooked over a drift-wood fire.

Haakon bent and pulled a handful of grass. It was a soft grass of such pale green as to be almost white, and fine sand fell from the roots. "We are at the tip of the land," Haakon said. "We will find a more sheltered cove with clear streams and rich earth."

That morning they sailed down the peaceful, surf-washed coast and around the point of land. Edith's homesickness almost overwhelmed her as they passed a bare, rocky island.

The sailors scanned the shoreline for tall, straight trees. They were still of a mind to cut timber to take back with them to Greenland.

"It must be used for a boat," Haakon said. "To bring settlers to my kingdom."

Bjorn was near Edith and she heard him mutter, "I wonder that his head doesn't burst."

There was a perfect wind and the ship travelled quickly. Strange and lovely seabirds circled the islands they passed and at nightfall they anchored in a long fjord with a great white sandy beach. In the morning they went ashore; once again the sailors were singing as they disembarked.

Edith helped Signe catch fish and cook them for drying, happy to be on shore and busy. Signe looked like a queen, but what kind of a queen caught and cooked fish?

Signe seemed happier too when she was busy. She chattered on about the wide clear creek that ran down to the beach. They bathed in a pool in the creek and watched the gulls crying overhead. They saw many songbirds, rabbits, and a white-tailed deer. Near the creek tasty berries grew.

Several days passed. "This is a wonderful spot," Signe said one evening as they sat by the fire on the beach.

"It will be sad to leave," a sailor said. "Yet leave we must. They will be worrying at home."

"I shall come back." The sailor named Jon said. "I will bring my family and even my cattle and sheep."

"To live in Haakon's Kingdom?" Bjorn asked.

"To come here, yes." Jon glanced at Edith. "I have four children, the eldest being about Edith's age."

Edith exclaimed, "Oh surely you won't bring your little ones on the dreadful seas."

"They have a love for boats," he said with a smile. "They won't become ill like someone I could name,"

He teases me, Edith thought gratefully. I do believe the sailors are beginning to like me. She said, "I miss Greenland."

"I am sure my children and Asta will be content away from Greenland's harsh winters. The children could play by the water all year long." Jon laughed out loud at a memory. "My wife, Asta, scolded me for wasting wood until she saw the children playing on the swinging implement I made. I placed a driftwood plank over a boulder. The children sat one on each end and were able to swing up and down."

"And you, Bjorn?" Edith asked.

"You know of Fjola, and of how she died." Bjorn stared at Edith thoughtfully. "You are much like her. My boys are grown and hunt walrus with me and help with the cattle. We have many cattle and keep a servant to help my wife. I have prospered and am content." Bjorn then turned to the other sailor. "Think, Jon. Don't you wish to stay with the familiar? We have no knowledge of the seasons in this new land."

"The growth is varied and abundant," Jon replied. "It is a safe place."

They had just finished a supper of roasted salmon. Haakon picked at his teeth with a twig. "Why must anyone leave?" He asked quietly. "Build your huts first. Next year will be soon enough to bring settlers."

Water lapped softly on the sand, and stars were very bright overhead.

"My family must come before I am satisfied," Jon said.

Bjorn spoke up. "You think the beauty of this place has cast a spell, Haakon. It has only made us more lonely for those not here to enjoy it with us. Next spring will be the time to return with settlers, but I have no wish to be a part of your kingdom."

A very sad-looking sailor said, "I have dreamed of fire dragons on the sea. I will not feel at ease until we go home."

Olaf nodded toward Edith, "She will keep the fire dragons away."

"Certainly she will," Haakon said.

Edith wished Haakon would tell Olaf and the sailors who seemed uncertain that she was not a mysterious creature. Several of the sailors were laughing. "Come on, Edith," Jon joked. "Cast a spell!"

During the night there was a thunderstorm. The thunder roared from one side of the sky to the other, echoing in the hills and lighting the whole beach. In the morning Haakon claimed he had a message from another world. He said he had been told to stay in the bay, soon there would be another storm and again a voice would tell him what to do.

The sailors whispered together and Edith didn't know if they believed Haakon or not.

Timber was brought to the beach ready to be loaded on the ship. The air filled with the lovely scent of the fir trees and the sound of axes. Edith wished they could take the forest home with them. She dried some of the pretty flowers that grew in the woods near the shore and also collected seeds for her mother. She longed for and dreaded the trip home. Thoughts of the seasickness and discomfort and danger ahead clouded her enjoyment of this beautiful spot.

Edith heard the men grumble about the heat. At first she was delighted by the warmth but she soon missed the cool breezes that blew over the icecaps. With Signe she sought a shady spot to sit while they cleaned the fish they caught with ease. How little effort is required, she thought, and yet we are unsatisfied.

The men were quarrelling about a rabbit snare someone had set very close to the path.

"It was you, Larus," Olaf accused. "You are the only one who loops the twine twice like the Shore-ones do."

Larus turned his back on Olaf and said to Signe and Edith, "Gunnar is much improved." He nodded toward the forest edge where Gunnar sat in the shade, staring blankly into the distance. "He has been eating well of the broth you prepared, yet even in this heat, his skin is cold."

Signe and Edith shared the nursing with Larus so he might hunt, fish and gather wood with the other men. Today Haakon had persuaded the men to help him bring some choice timber down from the hill for a hut.

The girls were spreading fish on the rocks to dry for the trip home.

Signe said, "Haakon wants the timber to build a house with instead of using stones. If we winter here, we will need more dried meat. I do suppose there will be a winter."

Edith smiled. "Oh, Signe, how homesick you sound for drifts of snow and the freezing winds."

Signe said, with a look of surprise, "I suppose I am bored if things are easy. I even enjoyed the dispute over the snare. Who of the men has troubled to set a snare when fowl and fish and berries are so plentiful?"

"If only we had such abundance at home," Edith said and her lips quivered at the memory of picking berries with her friends.

"Haakon has a desire to build a settlement to call his own," Signe said. "Does he suppose I will forget Greenland when I have not forgotten Iceland?" For a minute or two Signe looked as if she wished very much for a glimpse of her homeland.

They spent happy hours washing and mending their worn garments. The sailors had a metal awl from Norway that they used to punch holes when mending a sail with skin-twine. With this tool the girls were able to refashion their torn clothes. Edith's mother had taught her to sew and she was amused to find Signe had never learned this craft.

"You may practice on my torn pocket, Signe, for I have no wealth to put in it, but do lace it on evenly, one day my mother will see it again."

"If this is such a wonderful spot, why is no one here? And why do the men argue?" Edith wondered. They had taken Gunnar a drink and returned to turn over the drying fish.

"There must always be a first explorer," Signe explained proudly. "We are first to explore Plateauland. If you stay, Edith, you will not be a servant. You will be my sister."

"My family comes before even you, Signe," Edith said firmly.

"I suppose . . ." Signe started, but then she stopped. Something caught her attention and she grasped Edith's arm roughly, pulling her behind some big rocks. "Sh!" she whispered. "Look out into the bay."

Carefully Edith raised her head and looked toward the sea. Her breath was drawn in sharply with fear. There were so many canoes, the bay looked black with them. Suddenly Edith did not expect to ever see Greenland again.

Chapter Seven

The two frightened girls crouched behind a big rock on the beach, holding their breath. There in the soft white sand before them were countless footprints made by the Greenlanders during the past few days. The strangers would be well aware of their presence.

More than a dozen narrow boats dotted the little bay. Even from their hiding place Edith and Signe could see the faces of the men in the canoes. They had black hair, broad cheeks and their complexion was somewhat like that of the Thule. The men were dressed in skins, and Edith saw they were armed with bows and arrows and axes. Edith decided she should not have doubted the stories she heard. Vineland was very real, and unless she was dreaming right now, the warriors were also real.

The Thule who traded with Edith's village were friendly and kind; Edith hoped these people were the same, but she feared they were not. Signe had travelled much and had met many people of different races, yet she whispered she did not know who these people were. She too was afraid.

As the strange warriors circled the Greenlanders' boat, they gave weird sharp cries. "War cries," Signe breathed.

"Oh, Signe." Edith gave a little moan of despair. "What can we do?" Edith's mind was jumbled with fright. "Signe, do you suppose they could be friendly?"

"We aren't going to find out. We're going to slip back into the woods and run as hard as we can."

Edith looked behind them. Between them and the woods stretched an open expanse of white sand. They might be able to creep across this sand unseen by the men in the canoes.

Slowly she and Signe moved across the beach toward the trees. Once in the shelter of the forest they ran. Edith found it impossible to keep pace with Signe's long legs. At last they halted near a tree that was bent in an arc over the trail. Signe said, "Hide deep under this bush, Edith. If you are very still, no one will find you. I must run quickly to warn Haakon."

Under the bushes Edith could smell the lovely forest. Only a short while ago the woods had seemed empty, now she felt surrounded. Far above her the branches of a huge tree looked like a giant spider web that she was caught in. She crouched, shivering despite the warmth of the morning. It was unusually quiet. Even the birds seemed to be hiding from the canoes. Then she heard the far-off yipping noises made by the men in the canoes. Are they singing, she wondered, or talking?

Before long, the men's cries stopped and she could hear the faint sound of the waterfall in the creek. Perhaps the canoes had been pulled onto the beach. In a short while she heard a new sound, the whispering of many feet moving along the forest trail. Edith pressed more closely to the ground. Through the bushes she could see only the feet and ankles of those who passed. She did not think to count them.

Even after they were gone she imagined she could still see them, so many shadows had passed over her hiding place.

She waited while the sun moved slowly across the sky, expecting to hear loud cries and the sounds of battle. The birds came back and started to sing. Perhaps nothing was going to happen after all. She stood up and brushed the earth from her clothes.

The long hours in hiding had made her dizzy and she staggered onto the trail. She would creep down to the beach and see if the canoes were gone. Am I imagining a woman on the trail ahead of me? She wondered, for the forest seemed to sway as if filled with forms. The woman had a broad face and deep dark eyes; her long hair had been smeared with grease and tied with a piece of red cloth. She was dressed in soft deer skins. When the woman smiled her whole face lit up, her eyes shining like two dark stones reflecting the light of many candles.

Edith wanted to cry. The woman was lovely, but oh so strange. Then Edith remembered that with her blond hair and blue eyes, she too must look strange. "What do you want?" Edith asked.

The woman was smiling. She put out a tanned hand and touched Edith's pale face and laughed. Edith pulled back. She did not think she looked funny. The passing of the army of warriors had left her much too frightened to want to smile.

This woman was talking and it seemed to Edith that she repeated the same strange words many times. She is excited, Edith thought, and she is confusing me with her unfamiliar language. The woman motioned for Edith to follow, pulling on her arm as she did so.

Edith walked with the strange woman into the forest. There was nothing else she could do unless she wanted to be dragged, for the woman was strong and kept a grip on Edith's arm. Before long they left the path and crossed a small field. After some time they were once again on a path winding through the trees, but far from the familiar route that sailors had used getting timber. The woman seemed at home in the woods but Edith found the presence of so many trees bewildering. She longed for the wide beach. Which way is it? she thought in panic. How will I find my way back?

The way was long and hard and after many miles it grew dark. At home she had sometimes been tired when her chores were done, but at the end of the long day she rested safely in her own home.

"I have a home," Edith told the woman. There was no hope she would be understood but she talked anyway. "You are strange. I don't wish to go with you. Can't you understand that?"

Edith grew almost too tired to stand. How many miles had they come, she wondered? Still, I should be thankful, it is better to be captured in this manner than to be chopped up by a stone axe.

By now it was very dark. They had come so far from the sea that she could no longer smell or taste it. She heard the strange call of a bird or creature she had never heard before. It repeated itself time and again, "Hoo, hoo-oo, hoo hoo."

"What is it?" Edith cried out, but the woman took no notice.

Edith's legs grew so weary she could hardly move. Suddenly the woman picked her up and slung her over her shoulder. Edith was too tired to care that she was carried as if she were a bundle of furs.

"My whole body aches," Edith groaned, as every step jarred her thin body. "When will it end?"

At last they came to a place of torches and campfires. Through weary eyes Edith saw long buildings and many people crowding near. In the firelight all she could see of the faces was the slight glow of eyes. There was no glint of teeth, no smiles, and her hopes faded. Now it is certain, she thought, I will never see Greenland again.

Chapter Eight

After leaving Edith, Signe flew through the forest. Branches left red scratches on Signe's face and arms, but she could not pause. The lives of all her companions depended on her.

Twigs and leaves tangled her hair; roots tore her ankles and stones bruised her feet. Faster she ran, her breath like fire in her lungs. Oh why had the men come so far for these choice pieces of timber? Higher and higher their narrow trail wound. Today, she thought, we are all doomed.

Suddenly Larus appeared before her. "Signe! What has happened?" He called. "Is it Gunnar?"

She struggled frantically for breath, bent almost double. In the next instant Larus had turned and was down the trail.

She found her voice and gasped, "No," but he was already gone.

Haakon was the first at her side, even before the fleet-footed Erik and the rest of the crew.

"What? What? Signe, tell us," Haakon roared, as the

sailors all rushed to where she stood. At last she was able to gasp out her message to the sea of worried faces.

"There are many warriors. The water is alive with them."

"Are you harmed?" Erik asked.

"No, they were in boats," Signe puffed. "They have black hair. Their skin is like copper." Signe's voice grew steady. She was safe. Haakon was here.

"Ah," Haakon said with a laugh. "They may be the Simaba. They are painters and story tellers and no more warriors than your brother is."

"You know them?" cried Signe.

"Will they do battle?" Several men asked.

"I know of them. They like to make merry more than they like to fight, or so it is said." Haakon replied.

"You are wrong," Olaf said. "I too have heard of these Simaba, and they like to fight."

"It is all make believe," said Bjorn. "Haakon and Olaf can't know these people, for they don't even know what land we are in. We must make plans to keep watch."

"I see we have a new leader," Haakon scoffed.

"We can't fight them," Signe said. "There are too many. There must have been about thirty canoes. In each canoe were five or ten men."

"You wish to hide?" Olaf sounded astonished. "Never!"

"How many men are in the canoes, Olaf?" Haakon asked. "Are you wise enough to calculate the total?"

"And how am I to multiply both thirty by five and thirty by ten and come up with one answer," Olaf replied sullenly.

Signe said, "Forget your quarrels so we may save ourselves."

Signe was afraid the men would rush off to fight. She heard a chorus of warlike talk going on around her.

"Let us have a quick vote," Bjorn said. "If it is to be battle, we may be able to surprise them."

"Battle!" said Olaf gleefully.

"Battle!" said Haakon without hesitation.

"You are for battle, Haakon?" Signe asked. "We only have a few axes and knives with us."

Erik said unsteadily, "I think we must fight, Signe."

"Then it is decided," Olaf said. "We will do battle."

At Olaf's words the men looked surprised.

"There are many more votes, Olaf!" Bjorn said, "And I vote no."

"And I."

Signe was greatly relieved to hear the sailors' reply repeated over and over.

A voice called out, "I did not hear Larus vote. Where is Larus?"

"Larus is gone," Signe exclaimed with remorse. "Gunnar was on shore and Larus went to see to his safety."

There were concerned cries of 'Gunnar'.

The men were upset to realize most of their weapons were at their camp on the beach. Olaf was speedily distributing the few weapons they could gather together, so every man had an axe, knife or club. "Battle it is," he repeated eagerly, "We do battle."

As they hastened over the path leading to the beach, Signe could hear Haakon curse the sailors for being too slow and for the way they held their weapons. How do they endure it? Signe wondered.

Thoughts of Gunnar and Edith were tumbling through her mind like a skin canoe over rapids, when a sudden noise made her forget them. It was a drumbeat, rousing in its intensity and came from she knew not where.

The small party stopped so suddenly they stumbled against each other.

Was the drum behind them? Beside them? Above them?

Again it came, an even greater pounding. Loud . . . slower . . . softer . . . came the mysterious signal, like a drum and yet unlike.

They crouched in the brush with only the glint of weapons visible to Signe. I have only a club, Signe said to herself, Olaf gave me a club! It was not even a very good club. It had a very rough prickly spot for the handhold, and a bend at the end that made it difficult to wield.

Erik crept up to Signe's side. "I think they are above us," he whispered.

"Hush!" Signe feared his prattle would make them targets.

"Painters and storytellers, are they?" Erik muttered.

There they remained on through the afternoon. Birds sang and a hare nibbled twigs near them. Haakon crept through the heavy foliage to where Signe knelt. "This is the club Olaf gave me," she whispered, still annoyed. "It is all I have to fight warriors that can enter into the trees."

"Some hours have passed," he said softly. "I have passed the word to continue to the beach."

Signe stood with difficulty. She and Edith had worked at many tasks since dawn and she was very weary. What of poor little Edith? Signe wondered. How I regret not telling her to follow on after me.

The group had started down the path when the drumming sound assailed them once again.

Haakon raised his long knife and called, "I must see my opponent!"

Signe pulled on his arm and with their companions, they sheltered under the branches. The odour of crushed leafage filled the air. From where they crouched she could see the strange arc of a slender tree bending over the trail. Why this is near the very spot I left Edith! she thought. Where has she gone? Was she captured? She trembled with fear as she thought of her lost friend.

The drum beat loudly, paused, and did not come again. The crew waited, still and silent. The next move must be their enemy's.

With darkness came the insects that had not troubled them near the ocean breeze and by their camp fires.

Signe whispered, "What are we to do? How can we be rid of these distracting pests?"

Could Haakon be asleep? Signe wondered, for she was tormented, and when she tried to escape by burrowing under leaves and twigs, she found it only increased the fierce attack. It was near dawn before she slept.

"Hsst," Haakon woke her. "We will go to the spring to ease our thirst."

"I must find the spot where Edith was hidden," Signe told Haakon.

As she searched she realized her task was impossible. When in hiding the men had crushed the foliage on both sides of the trail.

"If she were near, she would join us," Haakon said.

"You are right," Signe sighed. "She is not here!"

Signe leaned for a moment against a giant dead tree and looked up to its top against the blue sky. The trees of this land were so amazing, surely they never would grow like this if there was winter,

Directly above, the familiar drumbeat rolled out, loud . . . slower . . . slow. This time the sailors rallied around Haakon, their weapons ready.

"He is in this tree," Haakon growled. "Now, I will deal with him!"

Knife in hand, he began to climb the tree, but the dry branches cracked under his weight and he crashed to the ground in a shower of bark.

A spatter of woodchips hit Signe's face and she looked up. "A bird!" she gasped. "Haakon! It is but a bird, black and white and almost as long as my arm! Stand here and see."

The flaming red-crested head moved rapidly back and forward against the wood.

"What a peculiar sight," Signe exclaimed. "It is like a hatchet. It will destroy its own head."

Over their heads the huge bird flew giving a cry of "Kik-kikkik-kik-kik."

The group refreshed themselves at the spring where water tumbled out of the rock and spilled onto the grass.

Signe studied her companions as they drank and washed their itching arms. Crestfallen, haggard from loss of sleep, rubbing and scratching insect bites, they were a sorry sight. Most of their weapons were scattered carelessly on the grass.

Olaf turned with one of his rare, stiff smiles. "It was a good omen," he said cheerfully.

"What was?" Asked the sailor Ivar, who was washing blood from his neck and a swollen ear.

"The spirit! The flaming crested spirit! It has brought us power for battle. It . . ."

"Never mind!" Haakon snapped.

From a clearing at the edge of the forest they were able to see the beach. "But I saw so many!" Signe said, and she looked up and down the bay. There she could see about two dozen of the warriors standing near a few canoes pulled onto the beach. Where have the rest gone? Can this be all? Is there to be an ambush?

As they drew near to the strangers, they stood

straight and looked as fierce as they possibly could. The strangers formed a loose circle around them, and pointing at themselves repeated over and over, "Simaba." No matter which way the Greenlanders looked, they saw the unsmiling faces circling. Haakon walked right through the ring of Simaba.

They moved aside for him and the ring closed again.

Surely the rest of the warriors must be nearby, Signe worried, and aloud she said, "Beware!"

Haakon walked toward where the Greenlanders had camped on the beach. The Simaba followed Haakon in a line as if following on a forest path.

"Good for Haakon," Olaf said. "He is leading us to our camp. We can get our weapons and victory will be ours."

Signe's frustration grew. "I tell you there were many men in the canoes and they chanted war cries."

By sign language the Simabas showed the Greenlanders that the fresh meat in their canoes was meant to be shared. The sailors began gathering firewood and soon had large fires blazing on the beach. Signe could see the sailors were enjoying themselves. They shared laughter and chores with the Simaba as the meal was prepared. All thought of war seemed to have fled as the tasty meat was eaten. Do they not remember their missing shipmates? Signe pondered. She was very troubled.

Signe signed to the Simaba and they gathered around her. They listened and watched as she showed them Gunnar's empty spot, his sleeping robe and the skin cup from which he took water and broth. They listened when she described Larus and Edith with signs. Then they talked together and signed in a way that baffled her.

Signe called Haakon from the feast and urged him to try the Thule tongue he learned as a child.

"Signe, you waste my time," he said. "This feast is of use to me if I am to rule these people."

"It's for Edith," she said, and when he was unmoved added, "And Larus and Gunnar."

"I'll try," he said crossly.

As the talk went on in many tongues and with much mime, the sailors and the Simaba laughed uproariously. Finally Signe sat down on a rock with her head in her hands. She was as close to weeping as she had ever been in her life.

Although it was growing late, Signe searched the woods with Erik and Bjorn, calling for their missing friends.

Night approached. Signe stared into the sinister depth of the dark forest, the sun was now only a faint glow on the tips of the trees. Edith was lost in there!

The Simaba talked excitedly and pointed into the forest. What can they see, Signe wondered, it is too dark to see anything? Can it be Edith at last?

As she crossed the sand, she saw that the figure coming out of the shadows was not Edith, but Larus. He was a pitiful sight, his garments were dirt-encrusted and torn, his face bloody from branch scratches and insect bites.

Larus stopped by the remains of the banquet. The men were silent.

Is it guilt that stills their tongues, wondered Signe, they have scarcely given the missing ones a thought since the feast was prepared?

"For shame!" Larus said quietly, for he had never been a man to raise his voice. "Have you forgotten your friend, Gunnar?"

"Is he dead then?" Haakon asked.

"He wandered from the camp but I lost his trail. I could not find him." Larus sat down in a heap. "I am not used to such a woodland. It is almost impossible to move through the growth!"

Larus' return stirred the men to action. Plans were made for the next day. Those who refused to enter the woods for fear of the unknown spirit in the form of a great drumming bird, would load the boat and prepare it for the trip home. A second group would search for Gunnar and Edith. Signe was to be in the third group who would go to the Simaba's nearby camp on the shore.

In the morning Signe took her place with Haakon in one of the birch bark canoes with the feeling they would find Edith at the Simaba's camp.

It was on this short journey that Haakon told her of his plans for Plateauland. "We will return in the spring," he said.

"We are going home then?"

"I think we must. Men are needed to govern my kingdom and they will not come without their families. We also must bring sheep and cattle for wool and milk. I will learn the Simaba tongue."

Signe thought about this and was agreeable even to his being king of Plateauland if this could be done peacefully. "How will you learn a new tongue while in Greenland?"

"We will take two Simaba children with us. When we return to Plateauland, they may stay in Greenland to teach more settlers."

"What if this is not permitted?" Signe asked, already filled with misgivings.

"Then we will capture the children," Haakon said calmly. "Adults would be troublesome. We must have children."

"Capture!" Signe cried, half rising. The Simaba at the paddles shouted at her in alarm. She had nearly upset the canoe.

Haakon nodded and she saw his jaw set stubbornly. His plan is treachery, she thought, it will endanger all our lives.

To add to her fear was disappointment. There was no sign of Edith when they reached the skin tents the Simaba had set up on the shore.

Chapter Nine

When Edith was carried into the village, she was all but unconscious and immediately fell into an exhausted sleep. She woke to find herself in a hut of skin and bark, surrounded by smiling women. They touched her hair and spoke in a tongue that rose and fell, but held not a familiar word. The air was filled with the odour of herbs and animal skins. Edith's first thoughts were of Signe. Was she safe?

Edith did not feel threatened by these people who called themselves Simaba. In a very short time she determined by their caresses and their care that her arrival was a special event for them. The lodges seemed to be inhabited only by women, children and old people. Edith knew the absent men could be hunting, fishing, exploring. They may well have been the men she watched while hidden in the brush.

At first she thought she would stay with Trefoil, the woman who took her captive, but she was moved to a bigger lodge. There she was to live with two ancient women and with Nighwillo and Sil, two young women.

The old women, Tha-awa, and Shu-shu sat all day sewing and weaving and laughing with the small children they tended.

Nighwillo and Sil seldom left her side. They brought her water to wash in, prepared her food at meal time, and were forever busy with a shell comb, working the tangles from her long blonde hair. With their hands they brushed at her garments, and with green branches they fanned away smoke and insects. Before many days Edith was very, very tired of Nighwillo and Sil. Even as she walked near the forest's edge looking for the path that could mean escape, the two were but a step behind her.

When she was able to avoid their attentions, she would work alongside Trefoil. Shelling nuts was a new experience for Edith. Trefoil showed her that the nuts were a type of fruit from trees. Edith put several of the rough shelled nuts in her pocket to take to Greenland.

Her feelings for Trefoil were mixed. Trefoil had taken her captive, yet with her, Edith felt no harm would befall her before her escape.

As she explored the village, she noticed a very old wrinkled man. He had a rosy olive-brown complexion that was neither like her own nor like that of the Simaba. His hair and beard were thin and his nose more like hers than his fellow-Simaba's.

When the old man looked up from the arrowhead he was shaping, she felt his gaze. It went straight to the lonely, secret spot in her heart where she kept her parents, and Ronaald, and now, Signe. She felt a shiver race through her and moved on quickly.

Having a sound night's sleep was at first a problem. The old ones, Tha-awa and Shu-shu, both snored loudly. The night air was also filled with the smell of skins and reeked of the balm Tha-awa made over the campfire to rub on her aching limbs. Choking smoke from the wood fires bothered Edith the most. It was supposed to go out the hole in the centre of the roof, but mostly it did not.

When they walked to the creek to wash, Nighwillo and Sil went to get herbs for Tha-awa from the medicine man, Weswen. While they were busy, Edith gathered flat stones and skipped them at the widest part of the creek. It wasn't long before a small group of staring children joined her and cheered her on.

For a short time Edith lost herself in the game. She was back on the green coast of her homeland with ice-coated mountains rising in jags behind her. The creek became a pool fed by a glacial stream and the voices were those of Kirsten, Anna and Margret.

When at last she tired, the Simaba children took her place. Eight, nine and even ten times the stones bounced until they hit the far bank. They are much better at the trick than I am! She puzzled. Why did they cheer me? Is it their custom or am I treated special? She found it tiresome when she was shown favouritism on the playing field as well.

However she had fun when she played with the tiny

children, for they scolded her if she was clumsy. They would shake their chubby fists at her, their round faces flushed with anger. Moherb was a cheerful little boy of about four. He liked the *circle game* and would play it with Edith. The players leapt between large circles drawn on the ground and then over a pole hurdle. Edith didn't know the rules of the game, and Moherb was too small to jump out of the rings, let alone over the pole, yet it was a game they never tired of sharing.

One afternoon Moherb was running through the brambles and scratched his arm. The women and girls on the playing field came, one by one, to console the crying boy. Before long, though, they tired of his cries and chanted a name at him.

"I suppose you are calling him 'baby'," Edith said angrily, and she sat down by her favourite to wipe his tears. Edith discovered that the source of Moherb's distress was a huge burr caught in the fabric of his tunic. With the burr gone he was once again all smiles. The Simaba girls acted as if Edith had used magic powers on Moherb. Do they think I'm an unearthly spirit, she wondered, like Olaf and Haakon did?

Moherb brought his sister, a shy girl named Lyretre, to see the person who had cured his arm. At that moment Edith was shedding a few quiet tears over the number of days she had been held captive. As each day passed she recorded it by putting a mark on the wall with a piece of charred wood from the fire. Tha-awa and Shu-shu never cleaned away the marks or anything else for they were an untidy pair and did not even wash their food bowls. Nighwillo and Sil constantly brushed at everything. Sil was wiping away the charcoal marks as Moherb and Lyretre entered the lodge.

"Why do you do that?" Edith cried. "Stop! Stop! I must know the day." Her eyes filled with tears. It had been a week! Had they sailed without her? "Will I ever have peace from these questions!" She gasped.

A soft hand took hers and gentle Lyretre led her outside and to her own crowded lodge. Lyretre pointed to the post that held the hide hanging over the entrance. There in charcoal, were seven marks.

"Oh, Lyretre." Edith squeezed her hand. "You understand."

Lyretre put a mark for day nine by her door the same day the hunters returned. Edith wished to help the women and children prepare the meat and hides; it was a job she knew well, but her captors insisted she go to the playing field where some of the very old and very young watched the men playing the *circle game*. Nighwillo and Sil seemed overjoyed to be watching instead of cutting meat.

She noticed one man in particular because he wore fringed attire and many beads. When he ran at the hurdle to jump, he tripped and did no better than Moherb would have. The other players showed him favouritism, and tried to put him first, but he shouted in anger and would not go. Moherb and Edith laughed for he did look absurd.

Later she saw this same man followed by two manservants whose duties appeared to be to serve him his meals and make him comfortable on a mat. It was obvious that he was a person of importance in the village.

"I wonder," Edith said to Nighwillo. "If that man finds his servants as irritating as I find you and Sil."

To Edith's surprise the young man came to where she sat after the evening meal and pointed at her saying, "A-dit," and at himself, "Tantan."

"You have a silly name," Edith said, enjoying the little joke with herself.

As Nighwillo and Sil talked to Tantan, they giggled and wiggled their shoulders and hands. Edith watched and thought, if Tantan is a prince, he will want a princess for a wife and not one of those two.

The next day Edith went with her two ancient housemates to the creek and they waded together, Edith, Tha-awa with her aching bones, and Shu-shu. How they laughed and splashed like children until Tha-awa nearly toppled over. "What fun!" cried Edith. "Are you having fun, Shu-shu?" she asked, for Shu-shu looked very tired and yet turned to Edith with a happy smile.

Later in the day the women dressed Edith in a soft skin garment they had sewn for her. They did not wish her to keep her old dress but she hung on to it, finally thrusting it under the sleeping mat. Her mother had woven the dress and fashioned the little overskirt with its big pocket. Even the pocket was special, for Signe had mended it.

The previous evening was one of storytelling, drums, and dancing by the flickering fires. Some new entertainment was planned as a high stage of poles was built on the edge of the field. A pole ladder was fastened to one side of the platform.

Edith was astonished when some of the elders escorted her up the ladder to the fur-covered seat placed there.

She watched in amazement as the crowds gathered, and fires were lit around the field. Before long dancers were moving to the beat of the drums and the pipe of whistles. She looked down on the brightly painted shields the dancers carried and saw the sway of the wooden beads they wore in strings about their necks, arms and even their waists.

The chanting dancers made a pathway for Tantan as he crossed the field carrying what looked like a crown made of white water lilies. Edith felt a surge of panic rush through her. If only I could ask what they want of me, perhaps I would understand, she thought. Why am I the one up here?

Then it came to her. They meant to marry her to Tantan! She shook with fright. This must be stopped.

The chants changed from a jumble of words to something that sounded like, "Zing — encess . . . Zing — encess . . . " Over and over the chant came until

Edith's head throbbed with the drums and she fancied she heard, "Viking Princess . . . Viking Princess . . ."

Thoughts stormed her mind: How afraid I am. It paralyses me. On the sea I had Signe but here there is no one. Unless . . . and then she remembered her new friends.

Standing, she tried to see beyond the dancers. Dusk was gathering and the fires made strange shadows everywhere.

"Tha-awa!" she called, barely able to hear her own shout above all the noise. "Tha-awa! Shu-shu! Help me. Make this stop."

From where she stood at the edge of the fur-covered platform she saw Tantan start up the ladder, moving slowly and still carrying the lilies.

Over the heads of the swaying dancers Edith looked for a path into the forest . . . she must get there . . . somehow. Then she saw him clearly. There he was, standing in the firelight. She was saved!

She raced to the ladder and clung to it with courage and strength, almost upsetting Tantan as she descended.

Down she went, rung by rung and pushed her way boldly through the dancers, calling, "Gunnar! Gunnar! It's me. It's Edith."

Beyond the campfires not a soul stood in the prancing light.

"Was I dreaming?" she asked softly and was surprised to hear her own voice. The noise was gone, and even the threatening chant of "Zing . . . encess," was quieted; the drums were still.

Slowly, very slowly, still feeling threatened, she turned. It had grown so dark the people who now crowded the platform with Tantan were formless. The Simaba near Edith stared to the east where, above the trees, Edith saw a great moving cloud. Beneath it another cloud hung, its darkness even more menacing.

It was not long before the storm hit with monstrous force. In her corner of the lodge Edith lay trembling as she listened to the sound of broken branches and debris hitting the walls. Trees cracked and fell with a thud, the noise muted by the wind. Water ran in the smoke hole of the roof.

The injuries from the storm were few, although most of the lodges were damaged. She was thankful to see a huge tree had fallen across the platform at the edge of the field.

The Simaba busied themselves trying to restore order, and even Nighwillo and Sil forgot to keep an eye on her. Edith was free to roam at will and searched the lodges one by one. Gunnar was not in the village, she felt, as she emerged from the last hut. Then what did I see? A spirit? She puzzled over that. If the *Signe* sailed and was swamped in the storm, that might explain Gunnar's spirit appearing to her. "If only I could talk to someone about this," she said out loud.

In a little clearing untouched by the storm she sat on a tree trunk and listened to the birds. There was one of every colour and a song for every mood! Where did they go in the winter? Her father said he believed they must dig holes in the ground and sleep until spring. Gunnar said that was wrong; they dived under the water and swam to a warmer climate. The answers she'd been given only made the riddle harder.

She heard the brush snap behind and knew someone was near. Moherb, perhaps, or could it be Tantan? She grew cold. Then she remembered something more frightening. A few days before a black bear had come into a field where she and Trefoil were picking berries and they fled, leaving their basket.

She leapt up ready to run.

Sitting on a tree root was the very old, very wrinkled man who had a nose a little like her own. She saw his beard was cut quite short and was as white as his thin, long hair. His beard? Why hadn't she noticed this before? The Simaba didn't grow beards.

"Norse?" She asked shakily.

He nodded. "I am Sigurd. Greenlander."

"It is so good to hear my own language!" Edith exclaimed. She stared warily at Sigurd. Who is he and why has he not spoken to me before? she asked herself. In spite of her misgivings she managed a smile, "Are you a captive too?"

For a moment the old man showed surprise, "It may seem to you as if you are a captive, but to these people you are a princess — Princess A-dit. As for me, I am a free man."

"How did you find your way here?"

"It would take many years to tell," he said. "I gave up my own language but after I heard the Viking Princess speak, I began to think in my native tongue again. Yes," he told her with a little smile, "I was the one who taught the Simaba to chant 'Viking Princess'."

"You never talked to me," Edith exclaimed. "I needed someone to tell me what was going on . . . To help me escape!"

"Escape from what? The Simaba love you. I have heard nothing but rejoicing since your arrival."

"None of this makes sense," Edith said.

Instead of explaining his remarks, Sigurd gave her his story. "I was not yet sixteen when I set out with a boatload of Norse explorers to try to find the settlement founded by Lief Ericsson. My companions were lost on a rocky shore, but I was saved by the Shore-ones. I lived with the Shore-ones for years, and married, and raised children. Then a storm caught our canoes as we returned from the hunt. I don't know if all died, only that I drifted for many miles to a strange shore. After years alone I joined the Simaba."

"How I wish you had talked to me, Sigurd," she said.

"I talked to your people."

"You did!" She greeted this with amazement.

"I left a snare on their trail so they would know they were not alone. Was that not enough?"

"Will you take me to the shore?"

He shook his head. "Today I feel too tired to care about Greenlanders. Now I am Simaba. You will be Simaba."

"I do not wish to remain here," she said. "Please help me escape!"

"It is possible your powers are hidden from you," Sigurd told her and went on in his rambling way. "There was a time when the winters were long and fierce year-after-year and the Simaba suffered famine. A wicked medicine man cast a spell on the king so he too became evil and quarrels and wars followed. One summer day a band of hunters came upon a deer and as they attempted to draw their bows, their hands and arms would not move. With hope that power would return to their arms they tracked the deer and were led to the sea." As he came to this part of the story Sigurd paused and smiled as if he looked on the wondrous scene that was said to have greeted the hunters.

He continued, "The sea was so pale it was scarcely blue and no motion rippled its surface. Although there were clouds overhead and trees nearby, no reflections were in the water. Like a small whirlwind a coil of mist rose from the sea and out of this haze emerged our blond princess.

"Prosperous times came to the Simaba villages from the moment the hunters returned home leading the deer with the blond princess riding on its back. There came a day many years later when the princess said, 'It is time'. When she was questioned her reply was, 'I will return'.

At once a swirl of dense vapour swept her away until . . ." Sigurd closed his eyes and nodded.

"Do not fall asleep!" Edith said, "Finish the legend."

He blinked his old eyes and stared at Edith, " . . . until you returned, Viking Princess."

"Of course this is nonsense," Edith said, "but I now understand why I have been treated so strangely. Now you must explain to the Simaba that I am a Greenlander."

Sigurd shook his head, "Since the day Trefoil went by herself in search of herbs and returned with you instead, our village has overflowed with happiness and good fortune."

"They think I am the princess," she said crossly.

"This I also believe," he said.

"Please tell them I am not their princess," Edith begged. Now she understood the feast and the crown of flowers. "I knew nothing of this legend. I thought they wanted me to marry Tantan."

Searching for the words he told her Tantan loved kindly little Lyretre and wished to marry her when she was grown. Tantan had told the Simaba council he would crown Edith as a princess and nothing more.

"I am tired." Sigurd leaned against the tree he was sitting under and was soon asleep. Somehow I must persuade him to help me, she thought as she started home.

When Edith returned to the lodge, she saw Shu-shu expertly lining a hide with fur. So the sailors were wrong, there would be a winter in Vineland. Her attention was drawn from Shu-shu's skilled hands to Nighwillo's clumsy efforts to fashion some sort of a carryall for her shoulder. Why, she is using my wool dress, Edith thought, in anger.

She snatched the dress from Nighwillo and looking desperately for a place to hide the treasured garment, rolled it tightly and held it against her heart.

With tears of frustration, Edith ran into the compound. Lyretre, Moherb's sister and Tantan's betrothed, was the first person she saw.

Suddenly all the emotion and frustration were too much for Edith. With scarcely a thought she thrust the bundle into Lyretre's hands. "Take it," she choked, and turned away, for she now felt she must become accustomed to this life. Like Sigurd, she was to be Simaba.

Every day she tried to elude Nighwillo and Sil so she might help dry the meat or pick berries with Trefoil. Each day it grew easier, for Nighwillo and Sil seemed to have tired of her since the hunters' return.

Sigurd was hard to find and did not care to talk. What a disappointment he was.

One afternoon, overcome with a desire for conversation, she sat next to him where he worked, making an axe. "I must tell you of the spirit I saw," she said, and told him of the sailor, Gunnar's spirit coming to her as he died in the ocean. He scarcely seemed to listen but it was better than talking to trees or stones.

"You know, Sigurd, I have told you how I miss my

family and Signe. Next to them I believe I miss dear old Gunnar the most."

The bleary old eyes turned to her at last. "Gunnar?"

"Yes. And now . . ."

"Gunnar?" He said slowly. "You mean the sailor with madness in his head? Weswen has brought his mind back. Weswen has been tending him so others would not receive the evil cloud from his mind."

Edith trembled from head to toe with shock. "He lives!" she said, breathless with joy.

*   *   *

All this while Gunnar had been with Weswen, the old medicine man camped near the creek.

Thin and dirty, but still her Gunnar, she found him by the creek. "I wish I knew why my head hurts," he said when he saw Edith. "Am I no longer on the boat? And why are you in this dream I am having, Edith Valgardsdottir?"

"Do you remember nothing?" she asked, kneeling beside him.

"I remember the storm. Since then all is a muddle."

She told him of his fall, and Larus' care. She told him, too, all that had happened on shore and he listened, looking puzzled.

"What I don't understand is how you came to be here in this strange land," Gunnar said, gazing about as if it was all new to him this very day.

She told him how she fell asleep in the boat.

"Poor Valgard," he said. "He will never guess where you disappeared to. Down a crack in some ice, perhaps."

"Oh, but Anna and Kirsten . . . ," she stopped herself, her cheeks growing pink. She hadn't meant to tell how her friends were involved.

When he heard his daughters' names he would not be satisfied until he heard the whole story.

As he listened, he held his injured head in his hands, and sat like that for a long while after the tale was told.

Suddenly he gave a roar of laughter and laughed until the tears came to his eyes.

"Those girls of mine," he gasped at last. "Those girls of mine."

Chapter Ten

The next morning, Edith was still thinking about Gunnar's response while she rubbed Weswen's ointment on Tha-awa's aching legs. The village was much noisier than usual and Shu-shu went out to see what was happening. When she didn't return Tha-awa struggled up and followed. Edith was last to go out the opening. There was a great commotion as the Simaba gathered as if for a celebration. What a welcome sight met her eyes amid that crowd! She trembled all over and ran toward Haakon calling, "I am here, Haakon. I am here!"

In a moment she saw Erik, Ivar and Olaf among the Simaba. The villagers gathered about them with laughter and exclamations. Erik's fair skin was rosy with excitement as Edith took his outstretched hand . . . but where was Signe? Her heart split into shards like the ice they chipped for water in winter. "Oh, Erik, who is here?"

"Haakon, Olaf, Ivar and Signe," Erik replied. "The others are at the shore with the ship . . ."

"Oh where is Signe?" She asked.

Edith need not have worried, for she soon found Signe in the centre of a crowd of admiring Simaba. Edith and Signe held onto each other and though they smiled, both had tears on their cheeks.

She clung to both of Signe's hands. "I am so glad to see you. I thought misfortune had come. Would you believe, dear Signe, I was becoming Simaba!"

The Simaba were stroking Signe's beautiful hair.

"They bother me like the insects." She laughed, but Edith could see her temper was being tested. The journey had been long and rough and hot.

When the travellers were rested, Signe and Edith sat down to talk, still surrounded by curious villagers.

"We never gave up our search," Signe said. "Even when it stormed. What a storm! It washed away the timber not yet secured and damaged the boat. We have spent all this time doing repairs. Even now those we left at the beach will be ensuring all is ready for a safe journey home. The Simaba who were camped on the shores left with the exception of two friendly families. Haakon wants to take some of them with us."

"How would they live?" Edith asked. "It can't be done."

"Already we know many of their words," Signe went on. "With the aid of signs we have learned much. Our Simaba friends found out that you were here, and they led us to you. Now we can all go home. The season for travel is passing and our seamen are afraid to winter here."

"Then let us leave right now," Edith cried, thoughts of her parents making her forget everyone else.

Erik came to them, smiling broadly. "They are going to have a feast before we leave. Let us share the entertainment and enjoy ourselves. We have met Sigurd. What great luck it is to find him here. He helped us talk to the villagers."

Edith said, "I am glad you like Sigurd, for I do too, though he would not help me escape. He believes I am a princess but you can tell him it's not so."

"Oh Erik," Edith sighed. "You are all beautiful. Even Olaf."

At this Signe laughed. "There is nothing that would ever change Olaf." She continued, "I can scarcely believe we found you! If only poor Gunnar had not wandered away . . . but you do not know . . ." Signe stopped, for Edith was looking at her with shining eyes and a bright smile.

"Signe," said Edith. "Let me tell you my news of Gunnar."

They were reunited with Gunnar that evening. He left Weswen's tent and joined the Greenlanders' camp in the village, but Edith returned to her own lodge. She would have Signe forever, but Tha-awa and Shu-shu were only to be her friends for a little while longer. If she ever returned, Moherb would be a man, and Lyretre would be queen, but the old ones would be gone. She took her sleeping mat to their side of the lodge and spent a nearly sleepless night listening to their snores.

The next day Haakon and Olaf met with Tantan and the Simaba council. Haakon said, "I want to make sure they understand my importance. They must be aware of the settlement I will build so they can use the winter to prepare for my return."

Edith heard Haakon tell old Sigurd to be prompt but at the appointed time he was nowhere to be found. Much later he was discovered asleep on a sandy knoll. Haakon poked him with his foot. "Get up, you useless greybeard! Move quickly now."

The meeting was held in the middle of the village with the talking lasting for several hours. Late in the afternoon Haakon was heard shouting for Sigurd who had wandered away and fallen asleep.

"Haakon has run into trouble," Erik murmured.

Edith sat close to Signe with Moherb and Lyretre snuggled beside her. At last Haakon came to them.

"Is it all right?" Erik asked. "Will they let us leave?"

Haakon wore a deeper frown than usual. "Yes, of course," he said, the irritation showing in his voice.

In the next few days the Simaba did little but prepare the feast for their guests. Signe had brought a few ornaments, ribbons, and other items for Edith to share with her friends. Edith visited all her favourite spots with Signe in tow. She had grown fond of old Sigurd. "Come with us back to Greenland, Sigurd," she entreated.

"No," he said. "I die Simaba. And you, too, Viking Princess."

Edith laughed. She laughed often now. "I'm going home, Sigurd."

Sigurd snorted. "I feared Haakon hadn't told you," he said. "The Simaba won't let you go."

Edith stared at him.

Signe took Edith's hand, "Come, Edith. Haakon will tell us it isn't so."

"You told them she can't stay with them, of course," Signe said when they found Haakon.

Haakon spread his hands, "What can I do? I didn't think it was that important. Of course they can not give her up. They believe she is the blond princess who promised to return and bring good fortune. She is an honoured guest and it is I who have been accused of trying to capture her."

Edith trembled.

They rose the next morning hoping to slip away with Edith. It was impossible. The feast and the visitors were causing so much excitement the Simaba were still roving the village at dawn.

"Please, Signe," Edith said. "Can you think of a way to persuade them to let me go home?"

Signe told the Simaba that Edith would bring bad luck. That was met with laughter. If Edith brought bad luck, why would the Greenlanders wish to take her with them? Or that was what Edith thought was said; old Sigurd was growing stubborn about translating.

"It is her colouring," Erik said. "Sigurd told us that

years ago a blond princess brought them luck. Perhaps I can convince them that all blond people bring luck."

Erik approached the council and by signs he showed he would stay if Edith could go. The villagers crowded about in great enjoyment. They poked at his short, bristly locks. They put fingers near his blue eyes which were squinty and bloodshot from too much sailing on sun-bright seas. They felt his tough, tanned skin and muscles. There was more laughter, and Edith saw Nighwillo and Sil encouraging the jokes. They teased Erik by making a motion as if to throw something away, and even held their noses as they laughed.

Edith felt her eyes fill with tears. "Thank you, thank you, Erik," she said.

Erik was shamefaced and looked miserable.

"I shall tell them I am the princess." Signe announced.

"Signe, do not," said Erik, horrified.

"It does not matter to me what country I am in," Signe said. "Life is good to me wherever I travel. It is important to Edith to return to her family in Greenland."

"Signe, give up this idea for now," Haakon said. "We will return in the spring and then we can trade the Simaba children we capture for Edith."

"Haakon," Signe said, looking directly at her husband. "Capturing Simaba would only bring death to us. Think back! When we first landed your plan was to stay."

"If we stay . . ." Haakon said, and paused, looking thoughtful. Suddenly he smiled and said, "I believe Tantan is a reluctant, slightly stupid prince. What they need here is a strong, thinking man for their king. You will be a goddess, Signe. We will have Sigurd to help with their silly language. It is decided. We will stay. You may go home with Erik and the others, Edith."

Once Haakon had made up his mind to stay he was quick to arrange a meeting to put his offer to the Simaba. A large crowd gathered as Sigurd explained Haakon's plans.

"Many of the villagers agree that if Signe stays, Edith can go," Sigurd told them, "But most want to know which girl is the true princess."

The Simaba council was to hold its own meeting and take a vote but it would be after the celebration. While the plans for this meeting were being made, Lyretre and Moherb cried and clung to Edith. Soon she was holding them too, and crying just as hard while she tried to comfort them with the few Simaba words she had learned.

That night huge fires were built, and dancers circled them as the food for the feast roasted. The flames cast shadows onto the trees as the drums echoed through the forest. Edith shivered, remembering the drums of another night. It was a noisy party under the bright stars; the night rang out with strange calls and shouts. Sitting near Signe, clinging to her arm, Edith was still afraid.

Edith had hardly taken a bite of her morning meal

when Sigurd joined them. In his halting way he told them the elders wouldn't meet until the next day. "To-day," he said, "Is for sleeping and for eating food left from the feast." All the while Sigurd was speaking, Edith gazed at Signe.

"I can no longer bear your sad eyes, Edith," Signe exclaimed and then leapt to her feet. "Come everyone," she said, "Today we learn the *circle game*."

Only Gunnar did not go with them. They found the campfire ashes had been scraped away and the involved pattern of circles redrawn on the hard-packed earth. When they joined the Simaba already on the field, Edith was the only one spared the jeers and teasing of the experienced players. How quickly my companions learn the game, Edith marvelled.

Signe was beautiful to watch, blonde hair flying, she played with energy and enjoyment. Olaf, thin and mus-cular and quick, made a sensation amongst the Simaba. Edith heard him chortle.

The summer nights in Vineland were not filled with light as were the nights of Greenland and even before they had tired, the players saw the shadows lengthen. As they ate by their evening fire Signe said with satisfac-tion, "We will sleep well."

"Sleep in our lodge," Edith begged. "I must know you are near."

"Tonight I will sleep at your feet," Signe replied, "And guard my little sister." She said this lightly, but Edith treasured every word.

The next morning the council sat for several hours talking little, and dozing a lot. Finally Sigurd wandered by looking for his chipping rocks so he could make arrowheads.

"Why doesn't that dull-witted ancient hurry?" Haakon complained. "I could shake him!"

Edith heard Olaf say, "We could play the *circle game* at home. It would make the winter less gloomy."

"Play that game?" Erik scoffed. "Why, we can scarcely get through the snow to tend the livestock!"

"We would draw the circles on the hut's floor," Olaf said. "Instead of the players jumping through the circles, we could toss buttons or beads. I will need to give thought to the pole vaulting."

Signe took Edith's hand and pulled her up, "Come have a game. Sitting here serves no purpose."

When the game players returned, they found the elders, who had been very still when they left, eating and laughing and talking.

"What is that about?" Haakon demanded of Sigurd.

"They must rest before they vote," was Sigurd's reply, and he settled himself nearby, his back against a sunny wall, and closed his eyes.

The usual crowd of curious Simaba surrounded the Greenlanders. Moherb placed a plump little hand on Olaf's knee. He talked earnestly to Olaf and then laughed and the Simaba onlookers laughed too.

"What did he say?" demanded Olaf. "Is it my face?"

Sigurd opened his eyes to tell him, "Moherb loves

children's joke-puzzles. He asked, 'Why did the arrow leave the bow?' And he answered, 'It was tired of being held back.'"

"And they laugh?" Erik exclaimed. "Why that is so stupid it is neither joke nor puzzle."

Olaf was smiling his stiff smile as he placed a hand on Moherb's head. "Wait! He is so young . . . Once I too enjoyed joke-puzzles."

Edith was so entranced by thoughts of Olaf as a little boy that she was slow to notice Tantan had arrived and was telling Sigurd something.

"Oh, tell us," she begged.

"The news is bad," Sigurd said.

There was a stunned silence and Edith realized that they must have all had the hope that everyone would be free to leave.

Signe's hands were clenched, "Don't despair, Edith. We will find a way!"

"Signe," Edith said in a small voice. "I do want to go home!"

"You don't understand, Viking Princess," Sigurd said. "The news is bad for *us*. We lose you. You may go home. Signe is to stay as princess," he sighed, "It seems, A-dit, that they do not know you are the real princess."

*   *   *

The goodbyes were many and Edith was scarcely able to speak as she left her new friends. Great hot tears rolled down Edith's face as she said goodbye to Signe. Erik looked as if he too was about to weep upon leaving Signe. "I shall look for you when I come this way again," he said. Signe embraced him and turning to Edith held her tightly for a moment.

"I shall watch for you," Signe said in a soft tone.

In the huge crowd of Simaba they seemed a very small defenceless group as they picked up their bundles to leave. Signe said each name softly as they passed her, "Gunnar . . . Olaf . . . Ivar . . .," and her voice trembled on the last two names, "Edith . . . Erik."

They were underway with Tantan's two manservants to lead them back to the sea. A few of the Simaba followed on the trail. Lyretre was among the last to go back, and just before she did she placed a rolled-up bundle in Edith's hands. "My dress," Edith gasped. As Lyretre turned back, Edith called after her words she had learned in Simaba, "*I will return*."

After some hours on the rough trail the little party of Greenlanders were exhausted. Abruptly their guides left the path and motioned the others to follow them down a steep, brushy embankment.

Gunnar staggered after them, "At last a chance to rest."

As Edith descended, she could hear the loud burble of a cascading creek. Two canoes were pulled onto a little bank beside the tumbling water, and near them were Sigurd and Tantan.

Sigurd gave them a quick, jumbled recital: "Tan-tan's servants overheard a plan to return Edith to their village. A group of Simaba are hastening along a short, rough route near your footpath and plan to waylay you where the trails cross. Tantan's men are going to continue on to try to make it seem you Greenlanders are still nearby."

"Two men speaking Simaba won't do," Erik exclaimed. "I will go."

"Erik," Edith faltered in alarm. "Think what you are saying."

"Don't fuss. I've had it in my mind to go back ever since I left Signe."

He gave each a quick smile and briefly clasped Edith who was shaking from head to toe with the shock of his decision.

As he bounded up the bushy rise after Tantan's men, she called to him in an unsteady voice, "Beware, brave Erik. Good-bye! Good-bye!"

"Quickly, A-dit," Sigurd exclaimed impatiently, as he pushed his canoe further into the water.

"It's not easy to fool a Simaba," Olaf said unexpectedly. "I will aid Erik. Good-bye little sea-spirit. Use your magic to guide the ship safely home."

Edith could only manage to choke out his name through her sobs. She wrapped her arms tightly about him thinking, this cannot be the same man who would have thrown me in the sea!

"Quickly," Sigurd repeated urgently.

As she splashed to the canoe, Edith had a final glimpse of Olaf, springing up the embankment with the same zeal he gave to the *circle game*.

"We are few . . . one canoe will suffice . . . Hurry," Sigurd urged. Tantan thrust paddles into Gunnar and Ivar's hands and with almost the same motion, he pushed Edith to the bottom of the canoe with their few bundles, and propelled the light craft through the turbulent water.

"I did not know we could navigate this creek," Edith exclaimed.

"Take heart," Sigurd shouted, "It is the seventh deadly wave that sinks a ship. There are but six rapids."

In an instant they were in the rapids, tossed high and toward slime-covered rocks; the paddles worked to keep them clear. After they narrowly escaped a second foamy boulder, Edith pressed her face against the bottom of the canoe. It throbbed like the sides of a living creature.

Stunned by the noise around her, Edith was shocked back to awareness by the mighty blows of the water propelling the craft.

There was a lull, a gentle bobbing came and Edith raised her head. Before her the stream narrowed suddenly, and descended between cliffs into a writhing channel. Instantly they were swept into the gorge and the spray blinded her. The next rapid seemed but a small disturbance in comparison and they glided with great speed into the pool above the waterfall. Edith and Signe had often bathed there and it was like a homecoming.

Since their arrival was anticipated by the crew, the ship was prepared for departure with the timber and supplies secured on board. For the moment there was time only for the briefest replies to the sailors' questions about why Signe, Haakon, Erik and Olaf were not there.

Anchors were lifted. Ropes were tightened here and slackened there. The sail was unfurled.

"They came," Edith heard Ivar exclaim and looking up she saw a full two dozen Simaba arriving on the beach, their spears raised.

Around her were exclamations from the sailors and Gunnar's voice, "Hasten, hasten. They mean us harm."

"If they dare to attack," Bjorn said, "The ocean will be red with their blood, not ours."

Edith heard murmurs of agreement around her. She trembled as she watched the Simaba, and when she saw Tantan approach them she cried out, "Can he stop them?" She saw the Simaba hesitate as Tantan called to them.

Edith dared not look back at the shoreline until the sail of the *Signe* caught the breeze and they were well away. The Simaba warriors were nowhere to be seen. Tantan was only a dot on the beach.

Chapter Eleven

When they made sail Larus set their course northeast by north. The wind was with them.

Gunnar was soon asleep and Edith looked for a place on the timber-crowded ship to claim as her own. She was very tired and wished to forget the events of the day for awhile.

Edith all but fell over Sigurd where he slept, looking a century old. She looked at him in disbelief. Why was he on board? She made her way to the prow and curled up on the robe Signe gave her on that other journey. When she woke hours later, the thoughts of Signe's kindness were still with her. Birds were circling the boat but when she sat up land was no longer in sight.

She heard Bjorn say, "So now you are a princess."

Edith looked about at the sea that didn't seem as frightening as she remembered. She then turned to Bjorn, "I found being a princess a great nuisance. It was as if I didn't own myself. I prefer caring for sheep." After some thought she added, "Bjorn . . . suppose I had not been on the voyage . . ."

"Don't fret," Bjorn answered in a gentle tone, "For some time we felt Haakon meant to stay in *Plateauland* and keep us with him. Signe and Erik are content with the adventure each day brings. As for Olaf . . . who knows?"

They were joking about the great bird that beat its head on trees when Sigurd woke up. His bleary eyes went from ship to sea and he exclaimed, "I remember!"

Edith said, "I didn't think you would come with us."

Sigurd wore his mischievous smile as he replied, "I may have the urge to travel. Iceland, Ireland, Norway and France are still out there somewhere, I suppose."

"France," Edith said. "I know nothing of such a distant land."

Sigurd continued, his tone now solemn, "This old *Simaba* thinks an ocean could scarcely be enough between himself and *The King of Plateauland*."

*   *   *

They had been some days at sea when Larus said, "I'm hoping for a harbour where we can put ashore for fresh water." The land was hidden by fog, but birds were everywhere, the smell of firs was very strong, and weeds floated on the ocean.

"Vineland food spoiled me," Jon said. "I could do with some duck eggs."

Some time later the fog lifted, revealing a great

craggy range of mountains that extended for many miles.

Larus said, "I am unsure. We had better go on. The Markland I know should not be on our starboard."

*   *   *

Before she reached home Edith decided *Princess A-dit* must be put aside forever. The first step was to creep under a tarpaulin and don her familiar woolen dress with its handwoven overskirt and apron. With care she folded the dress that had been sewn for her by Tha-awa and Shu-shu. What a nice surprise it was to find Lyretre had washed her old dress, and had thoughtfully put the bark envelope of seeds and the three tree-fruit back into her pocket.

Edith showed the hard-shelled seeds to Sigurd. "We often picked those nuts at home," Sigurd said, and Edith knew *home* for him was the Simaba village. He went on, "Their taste made me think of the butter we had when I was a child."

Edith knew how to use the oars, but she wasn't needed today as they navigated into a cove in a point of land that stretched out into the ocean. There was much excitement as they neared land for they could see what looked like buildings on the shore.

"Take caution," Bjorn said.

"There is no one about," Larus said. "I've been watching for some time."

113

While the boat was still being moored, Sigurd went ashore and crossed a beautiful meadow toward a raised level space. Edith leapt from the boat and ran after Sigurd in excitement. In a moment, spear in hand, Bjorn was beside them.

"Take care," Bjorn warned again.

"No one is there," Sigurd said. "It falls in ruins."

Edith heard the sailors shout in astonishment as they, too, came closer to the buildings. They were looking on the remains of a number of sod dwellings, three of them quite large. The sod roofs and even some of the walls had fallen, but one building had only slight damage to the wood frame.

Edith had lived all her life in a small hut, but she knew of many big buildings like this in her Greenland community. They could serve to house all the relatives of one or more families.

"Who built this?" Ivar exclaimed. "Surely these are Norse homes."

"Could this be Lief Ericsson's settlement?" Sigurd asked. "Ah, but it has taken me a lifetime to reach the place I sought so long ago."

The following days were busy as they filled their water kegs and set about replacing some of their food supply that was touched by a dusting of green mould. They caught salmon in a nearby stream and picked berries to be dried over the fire pit. Meals were delightful, but Jon found it was too late in the season for the duck eggs he longed for. The foggy and windless days gave them the excuse they wanted to linger.

Mostly the days were happy, but Edith never forgot they were still far from home. All was not perfect.

Larus grew restless. The wind blew north and he was anxious to take advantage of the good sailing. Some of the sailors wished to linger and go exploring. Bjorn led a party of the crewmen into the forests and they found fishnets in the stream and snares close by. Though no people were to be seen, the meadow on the cove lost its attraction as they slept nervously, their weapons beside them.

Before setting sail they looked for treasures in the ruins, but found little other than a few boat rivets and a broken fastener that may have been used on a cape.

"What do you think?" Jon asked his companions as they unfurled the sail and the wind caught the many diamond-shaped pieces it was made of. "Wouldn't this be a finer place to settle than Haakon's *Plateauland*?"

They were well away and the settlement hidden behind an island when Edith discovered that the washing Lyretre gave her dress had dislodged Signe's unskilled stitches,

"Oh Sigurd, the tree-fruit I showed you have fallen out a hole in my pocket! Now I only have the flower seeds left for Mother."

Sigurd had been watching that strange point of land disappear, "You shouldn't be looking back A-dit, you are so young. Look forward to the day when perhaps those lost nuts could split their shells and sprout in the ground becoming new trees in a new land."

*　　*　　*

Edith was wild with anticipation. Gulls and gannets screamed over the waters and the mountain peaks on the northern horizon touched the clouds.

Bjorn exclaimed, "At last I will be home and I need never again see a tree!"

Sigurd stared, seeming entranced, "I remember a longboat of warriors in that very fjord. I would have joined them if my father hadn't prevented me."

They were battling waves, but for once Edith didn't care about the seasickness that was coming to her. "I wonder if anyone on shore can see our sail," she said.

Larus turned to Gunnar, "We should have heeded that swell from the southwest. It gave us notice of this heavy weather."

Soon all hands were at the oars, even Edith and Sigurd. Oh, Edith thought, overcome with disappointment. We were almost home.

"Can we make landfall?" Sigurd called to Gunnar, and the gale gave answer.

The sky seemed to drop on them and they strained at the oars, Edith wishing for the three strong oarsmen they had left with the Simaba. Sigurd began to bail and Edith, now too ill to row, joined him. Together they could scarcely keep up with the deluge. After bailing for what seemed like ages, Edith realized they were being driven northwest, straight into the ice.

Beside her Sigurd shouted over the noise of the waves, joy in his voice. "I saw clouds hanging peak to peak across the mountains. I saw Greenland!"

The turmoil strengthened and no one tried to talk. As they rocked, Edith heard a loud snap and wondered if the cargo of timber was breaking free. The deadly load could easily founder them.

Again a great wave hit and she could hear the sailors counting . . . Not unlike a Simaba chant. "Three . . . Four . . . Five . . ." Sigurd had told her about the seventh deadly wave some sailors feared; it was said to be the wave that would swamp a ship.

Then as she heard "six," Bjorn called out wildly, "Goodbye my friends!"

On the waves came, one after the other. "This turmoil is not sinking us, but how sick it has made me!" Edith moaned to herself, and yet she kept on bailing.

As shouts of "Pull! Pull!" rang out, she saw a wall of ice next to them.

"It is grounded!" Shouted Larus, sounding almost happy.

What are they doing? Edith wondered, and then she saw the men had frantically pulled into the lee of the grounded iceberg and were mooring the boat to the ice. "Are we in a cove?" She asked.

"In an inlet, and it has saved us," Gunnar replied.

"How still it is now," she said as everyone joined in the bailing. They had been nearly awash.

Their woolen tunics were soaked. "It will be a long wait," Gunnar said as they shivered.

"Not as long as down there," Larus said, nodding at the water.

To Edith their position looked perilous, yet the sailors were joking and even eating. As soon as the seas calmed somewhat they were once again underway, working out to sea to avoid the coastal northerly winds. With the sun to warm her Edith fell asleep and did not wake until she heard shouts of land sighted.

"Are we near home?" She asked, standing up.

"Look ahead," Gunnar said as a perfect breeze guided them.

How beautiful Greenland looks, she thought, gazing at the sun-touched ice-caps.

Gunnar was looking at her and said with a grin, "I do believe that at last you have grown taller, Edith Valgardsdottir!"

Bjorn said, "Yes, she was very small when first we saw her."

There was laughter remembering that day so many long weeks ago when a small sea-spirit appeared among them.

As they sailed into the fjord, the sky, the crags and peaks were reflected in the water, and moving before them was a marvellous image of the carving on the prow. There she was, the beautiful Signe, hair flowing . . . Oh how I do miss her, Edith thought.

They shot into the wind to check their headway and then lowered the sail. The men took the oars.

At last the friendly cove took shape. Edith saw the cliff where her father's pasture ended. She saw a dark line across the cliff. It was the ledge where the sheep, Hela, had fallen. She could see her father's house and the houses of the village. She saw the green pasture. Greenland! This was her Greenland.

Then she saw someone in the pasture, someone who had been watching the sheep and was now moving toward the houses. Soon everyone would know the ship was returning. By the time the *Signe* reached the landing, a welcoming party would be there. Yet why did the figure cross the pasture so slowly? Margret! It must be Margret, her dear friend! She had been tending her sheep while she was away.

With a warm feeling of content, Edith thought, I am needed here. Very soon she would see her mother and father, and Ronaald and Margret, and her heart filled with joy.

She heard Gunnar's jovial voice ask, "I wonder how Erik and Olaf fare, and what of Signe?"

"Well, I don't doubt they're having the time of their lives," Ivar laughed. "The *circle game* seems so long ago!"

Larus asked of Gunnar, "More trips, my friend?"

"Yes, but it won't be the same without Haakon and Olaf," Gunnar replied.

Bjorn called out, "I wonder if Haakon the Hateful is now a king."

Edith had not forgotten those who had helped her. Even Haakon, who had threatened to kill her, had not been all bad. "Perhaps we can now call him Haakon the Great," she said.

Bjorn replied. "Perhaps just *Haakon the Not So Bad After All*."

Edith saw that Gunnar was taking care of old Sigurd. And what of Sigurd? she thought. If I feel like this, what can Sigurd be feeling?

Then Edith forgot everything except the people waiting on shore. She was now close enough to see the faces in the crowd. Among them she saw the happy faces of her mother and Ronaald.

"Where is Father?" She cried as she leapt ashore and rushed into her mother's arms.

"He comes," her mother said.

Edith turned to greet Ronaald and saw at last he was growing the beard he wanted!

And her father? Here he came, almost running, but why did he carry a pair of skis?

When clasped in his arms she asked him, "Father, why have you brought skis?"

"I made you a new pair," he said. "You will need them when we go walrus hunting together."

Over her father's shoulder she saw Gunnar's family

and Margret. Then she laughed out loud. Standing near them, as if she too were a person, was one silly sheep named Hela.

The Viking Princess
Historical Note

On the tip of the Northern Peninsula in Newfoundland, at a place called L'Anse aux Meadows, are the ruins of a Norse settlement, the only one of its kind in North America. The site was first discovered in 1960 by the Norwegian archeologist Anne Stine and her husband Helge Ingstad. It was excavated by a team under their direction from 1961 to 1968, and again by Parks Canada from 1973 to 1976.

Archeologists found that the site was occupied by Norse people sometime between the years 990 and 1050 AD. It seems these people did not live there for very long. If you visit the site today, you can see reconstructed Viking houses and workshops, and listen while Parks Canada interpreters tell you what life must have been like for those early Viking visitors. In one display case in the interpretation centre, among the Viking artifacts, is a butternut, what Edith called a "tree fruit." This kind of walnut grows far to the south of Newfoundland. It tells us that those Vikings must have travelled to the mainland of North America, or traded with others who did.